SLIM SIRINGO
'A BRIMFUL OF NETTLE'
BOOK #6

DAVID W. BAILEY

For information contact: info@outlawspublishing.com
Cover design by Outlaws Publishing LLC
Cover Art by Michael Thomas
Published by Outlaws Publishing LLC
July 2024
10987654321

Chapter One

A Sad So Long

With the threat of civil war creeping into the news and on everybody's mind those weapons would fetch a healthy amount of money. Back east, it seemed a dark cloud has risen and has perched itself over Washington, D.C. It seemed to be clouding the eyes and minds of those knucklehead politicians.

The southern states still rant, "If that backwoods buffoon gets elected, there will be war."

It never speaks differently of the matters in which the southern delegates made their decision to secede from the Union. Not one iota of the real reason for secession. Dissention has already reached the western states. Brawls are forever breaking out amongst the citizenry. Even amongst the ranks of the military, there has been a separation of states. Many have died from shootings, or being beaten, even hanged without the declaration of war.

Slim was angry about digging a single grave when the whole country was worried about digging millions of them.

Civil unrest will eventually lead to civil war was the word of the day. Many wives will be widowed. Many children will have no father. Brother will lose a brother. Fathers will lose a son. It will seem as though the whole of the United States will become one large graveyard. Americans fighting Americans. Family against family. It doesn't seem possible, and yet, there it is. The drums of war are sounding all over the country, and in every territory yearning to become a state.

The real reason for cessation was to protect the southern slave institution, and by creating their own country, they would not only protect their slave institution, but they would also protect what they considered their very own way of life. Even now, weapons are being produced in greater numbers than before. Southern gun makers such as, C. Chapman, out of Nashville, Tennessee, as well as, Churchill & Sons, out of Columbiana, Alabama.

Also, there was, J. M. Eason Brothers, out of Charleston, South Carolina, as well as, W.S. McElwaine, out of Holly Springs, Mississippi.

There were many more, but these are just a few of those many. Armories are stockpiled throughout both the north and the south. War! In 1860, what was known as the border states which were Maryland, Delaware, Kentucky, and Missouri, they knew that if Civil War did break out, the war would surely be fought on their soil.

So, the people of these states formed a new party, the, 'Constitutionalist Unionist' party. They stood for the Constitution and the Union. They tried to ignore the controversial issues that divided the country. However, the party did not last long. If they had lived long enough to develop a symbol like that of the democrat party, which is ... a donkey, or what the Republican party have as their symbol… an elephant. Theirs would most likely be an Ostrich with its head buried in the sand. In any event, it wasn't just that if Lincoln would win the election, but if any republican would win.

The democratic south has had, 'a brimful of nettle'. A saying that would travel the whole vast area of the United States. In other words, their cup is full and running over at being pushed around by the northern states, telling the southern states what they can, and cannot do. But by no means was the southern states the only ones suffering, 'a brimful of nettle'. The northern states also had their fill of the southern states telling the northern states what would happen if Lincoln won the election, or even if a republican did so, the south would secede and civil war would erupt on every front. The states continued to harass each other in the Senate, in Congress, and on the streets of America, and in doing so, anger erupted, deep aggravation, disgust, incensed behavior, deep rooted hatred for the opposing side. The people of the northern states, as well as, those in the southern states, have become utterly irritated to no end with no give from either side. The southern states are now crammed full with a, 'secede, civil war', attitude. A deadly attitude, but still, an attitude, nonetheless. But in the town of Comanche, Oklahoma, there is also a fight going on. The murders, fraudulent takeover of property, double dealing, raids on farms, and the killing of farm animals, including horses, and cattle to ensure a takeover of that farm.

The more people fought back; the more determined Devlin Wade was to put them under his foot, or put them six foot underground. He didn't care which came first. It was said, 'You may care how many died, but be rest assured, Devlin Wade does not care."

However, in the town of Waco, Texas, Brass Tacks, and a few of his men are in search of the wagon of weapons he sold to the three Irishmen. He wanted the guns back and those three Irishmen dead. He stared worryingly at the wagons that lined up and down the street.

Then, a man named Mark Jernigan asked, "Just where do we find your lady friend?"

Brass Tacks replied, "Who? Oh, you mean, Lilah? She works nights at the Dancing Bear Saloon on the other side of town."

Another man asked, "That's fine and dandy. So, where do we find your eyes and ears 'round here? And, don't tell me he works at the Dancing Bear Saloon too."

Brass Tacks answered, "You can say he works there." He smiled, then said, "But that's because he owns the place."

Thrilled, the man, then asked, "Does that mean free drinks, Lane?"

Brass Tacks replied, "Didn't I say he was a friend? We'll not take advantage of that friendship unless it's offered to us. Is that clear?" Getting no response, he asked again in a louder tone, "I said, is that clear?"

There came a scattered array of, 'Sure, sure.' to, 'Yeah, sure."

Brass Tacks, then said, "That's what I like to hear. Consistency."

Then, Cecil asked, "So, what do we do between now and then, Lane? I don't think the place is open, is it?"

Brass Tacks answered, "Not yet, but it'll open sometime 'round five, maybe six o'clock today, so until that time, we relax and enjoy the sights."

Paul, then said, "I sure am gittin' tired a sittin' 'round on my duff doin' nothin' but playin' tidily-winks, or playin' mumbly-peg."

Brass Tacks said, "Those are kid games. What happened to poker?"

Paul replied, "Lost the cards."

Brass Tacks chuckled, saying, "Now, how in thunder do you lose a deck a cards?"

Paul, then said, "Careless, I reckon."

Brass Tacks shook his head slightly, but said nothing else.

At the Etsy barn, Flynn, Seamus, and Clancy were worried about what happened to Casey O'Connor. He had not returned to the barn last evening. They left the barn in hopes of finding Casey stumbling his way from the Buckhorn saloon to the barn, completely scuttered, (blind drunk). However, that was not the case. They saw no sign of Casey. They entered the Buckhorn saloon to see if he was passed out on their floor, or slumped over a table.

They found he was neither. So, question is… where is Casey then?

Then, A.K. Masters walked into the saloon. He arrived in time to stop Flynn, Seamus, and Clancy from leaving the saloon. He directed them to sit at a table. So, that's what they did. They sat at a table near the swinging doors.

Sheriff A.K. Masters, then said, "There's no good way to say this, but to say it right out."

Flynn smiled, saying, "And, what would that be, Sheriff? We're here lookin' for our friend, Casey O'Connor. You haven't seen him, have you?"

Sheriff Masters replied, "He's the reason I'm here. You see…"

Flynn said, "Aw, now sheriff, what be the fine for bein' drunk and in the clink?'

Sheriff Masters, then said, "He's not in jail. He's at the undertaker's. He was killed last night and robbed."

All three men looked at each other with concern, and confusion.

Then, Flynn smiled awkwardly, saying, "Oh, now Sheriff. You must be jokin' us…"

Sheriff Masters answered, "I'm afraid not. His body was found early this mornin' in the alley between the barbershop and the saddlery shop. He was knifed to death. I'm sorry to have to tell you this. I know he must've been a good friend."

Flynn replied, "Aye, Sheriff, that he was. A dear friend. Thank you for tellin' us Sheriff."

Sheriff Masters, then asked, "He have family back in Ireland?"

Seamus answered, "No wife, nor kids, but a father what lies on his death bed I'm afraid. The last he checked back on him in Portadown, Ireland."

Sheriff Masters, then said, "That's too bad. I'm sorry."

Flynn asked, "Do ya mind if we go pay our last respects, Sheriff to a dear, dear friend?"

"I wouldn't think too kindly of you if you didn't." Sheriff Masters replied.

Flynn stared down at the floor, saying, "Aye. T'would be a terrible thing not to. Would it not?"

"Aye, it would." Sheriff Masters replied.

Flynn quickly raised his head, looked at the sheriff in surprise, then said, "Sheriff?"

"I grabbed a vernacular." Sheriff Masters replied.

Flynn, Seamus, and Clancy in unison, said, "Aye."

Seamus said, "That ya have, Sheriff. That ya have."

Sheriff Masters, then said, "Yes, well, I must be goin'. I have a town to protect, if I can." He rose, then stepped back from the table, he then walked to the swinging doors. He opened a section of the swinging doors, then he stopped. As he leaned against it, he looked back saying, "If last night was what I could look forward to with that civil war everybody thinks we'll soon be fightin', then God help this country." Tossing his right hand in the air, he said, "Well, I'll see ya."

Sheriff Masters left the saloon causing the swinging doors to swing back and forth. At the whooshing sound of the batwings, they looked at each other and frowned.

Flynn, then said, "Well, Lads, we have a sad thing to do this day."

Seamus replied, "Aye, that we do, Flynn, Darlin'."

Clancy rose from his chair saying, "Well, let's not doddle then."

As each man rose from the table, Flynn turned to Burl Matheson, owner and bartender, who stood behind the bar drying some beer glasses with a rag.

Flynn, then asked, "Could you be so kind as to direct us to the mortuary, Sir?"

Burl replied, "I heard what Sheriff Masters had to say 'bout your friend. That's too bad. You have my condolences."

Flynn said, "Thank you. The mortuary?"

Burl, then said, "Ah, yes." After clearing his throat, Burl said, "When you leave here, turn right. The mortuary is five buildings down on your left, across the street. You can't miss it. It has a big sign out front that says… uh, you can't miss it."

Seamus replied, "Thank you kindly, Sir."

Burl said, "You're quite welcome, Gentlemen."

Without another word spoken, the three men left the saloon leaving the swinging doors flapping in the wind, and Burl wiping down beer glasses. When they were outside the saloon, they turned right, and walked down the boardwalk.

They never noticed before, mainly because they wasn't looking for it, but yes, there was a rather large sign stating, 'McQue Funeral Parlor'. They stopped on the boardwalk before crossing the street, and stared at the mortuary with sad looks on their faces.

Clancy, then asked, "Well, shall we?" He stepped off the boardwalk with Flynn, and Seamus following. The street was somewhat crowded with horse and rider, as well as, different styles of wagon traveling main street.

Men, women, and children walking the boardwalk, causing the trio to stop to allow cross traffic. When they reached the mortuary, they stood staring at the building.

With eyes wide, Seamus, then said, "Tis quite ominous, ain't it?"

Clancy replied, "It's just a building."

Flynn answered, "Aye, Lad, but it's what's inside the building that seems ominous, and, I must say, quite eerie."

Seamus, then said, "The term, 'I walk with ghosts', now has a rather ominous meaning."

Clancy turned to Seamus, asking, "Are you a man, or a mouse?"

Seamus swallowed hard, then asked, "What kind a cheese ya got?"

Clancy replied, "Aw, jeez, come on fellas. Ya act like you never seen a dead man before."

Flynn, then replied, "Not one of our own, Lad. Not one of our own."

Clancy, then said, "Well, shall we, Gentlemen?"

When the trio entered the mortuary, they entered the anteroom, staring in awe as they stared wide eyed at the décor. Purple drapes hung on silver rods, eight to ten feet in length, three to four feet wide, just to stop and inch, or two from touching the floor. They identified three rooms, but for what reason, they had no idea. Just then, a man walked into the room from one of those doors.

The man asked, "May I help you, Gentlemen? I am the mortician, and owner, Ben McQue. Oh, I'm so sorry

Gentlemen. You must be here to pay your last respects to your friend? Sad that."

Flynn replied, "Aye, that we are, Mister McQue."

With a simple curious glance at each man, Ben, then asked, "You're not from around here, are you?"

Clancy replied, "No, sir, we ain't. Could you tell us where our friend Casey would be?"

Ben said, "So, that's his name? Normally, we have no idea who the deceased are, 'cept for maybe a friend, or a family member who tells us what their name is." Ben stared at the trio, then said, "I'm afraid I must ask, Gentlemen, but will there be a headstone, or just a wooden grave marker at grave head?"

Flynn replied, "No, no headstone. Just a simple grave marker to mark his passing, with his name of course."

Ben replied, "I understand fully." He turned, saying, "If you would follow me, please. I will take you to see your friend, Casey."

The three men looked at each other with an acute desire to leave the mortuary, but they followed Ben through one of those doors. It led to another room, where upon they found Casey. He was lying on his back on a rather narrow table. He was covered with a linen cloth that covered his feet to rest just at the shoulders.

Clancy asked, "Where are his clothes?"

Seamus also asked, "Yes, where are his clothes, and why have you draped him in such a manner as this? Tis shameful, I must say."

Ben replied, "I assure you, Gentlemen, that I was just preparing the body for burial."

Flynn, then said, "Are you plannin' to bury him naked? My good man, that is not…"

Appalled, Ben answered, "Oh, no, Sir. I would not disgrace a body in such a way as that. But I am merely washing the body. Cleaning it for a proper burial, then I will redress the body in his own clothes, and have him placed in the coffin, and then, the coffin lid will be nailed down."

With his face flushed, Flynn, then said, "Please, spare us the details of that."

Ben replied, "I am sorry. Feeling a bit queasy, are we?"

Flynn looked like he had just swallowed the canary.

Flynn, then replied, "Yes. Quite."

"I thought so." Ben replied. "It happens all the time. As I was saying, I was cleaning the body, preparing it for burial, and since the deceased has no relatives here, I felt it necessary to write, John Smith, on the headboard at graves head. I also thought he was alone in Waco with no friends. I am very glad you three have come in. I now know what to write on the grave marker."

Seamus, then asked, "May we be alone with our friend, Sir?"

Ben replied, "Yes, of course. If you need me just holler. I'll just be next door."

Clancy said, "Thank you. Mister McQue."

"Of course. My pleasure, Gentlemen."

Then, Mister McQue, the mortician, bowed slightly and left the room, closing the door behind him. Then, all three men turned to gaze at the body of Casey O'Connor. A dear, dear friend. The eeriness of this mortuary, however, was slowly creeping in on them. Suddenly, they felt closed in, and the walls had started to close in on them.

There was a tightness in their throats that made it hard for them to swallow. They kept looking back at the door, the only door to the room, expecting someone, other than the mortician, to walk in. To say they felt uncomfortable, was an understatement. The silence of the place was ear shattering. They would look at each other with worried eyes, as well as the door to the room with great uneasiness. Then, the door to the room opened, causing the three men to stare wide eyed at the door. They let out a heavy sigh of relief when the mortician walked in.

The mortician asked, "Sorry to interrupt, Gentlemen, but would either of you like to have a glass of brandy? I have found brandy calms the nerves while viewing the body of a friend, or a family member. Any takers?"

All three men replied with a, "no thank you", reply.

Clancy, then asked, "Is this place always this… still, and quiet? It's… rather spooky."

"Yes, it is." Ben replied. "You see, the dead can no longer speak, and seeing as how I am somewhat... demure, I rather enjoy the stillness. However, it is quite dis-pleasurable to others."

Flynn said, "That I can believe."

Ben, then asked, "Will you Gentlemen be stayin' for the funeral, or moving on?"

Flynn answered, "We'll be here, unless somethin' happens and we have to leave."

Ben said, "Well, Gentlemen, let's hope nothing happens to cause you to leave."

After Ben left the room, Seamus said, "I don't like the sensation when I'm around that man."

Clancy asked, "The sensation, Seamus?"

"Aye, Clancy." Seamus replied. "The feel. You know, I feel… dirty. Tis like I need a bath after bein' around him."

Clancy replied, "He is one strange cuss. I'll give you that."

Flynn answered, "Aye, Clancy, he is, but right now, we need to focus our attention on Casey, and not on the mortician. Casey was our friend. That man is not."

Without another word, their attention turned to Casey, lying on a table, covered in a sheet.

Flynn, then said, "There had to be more than one, Lads. Casey could handle his own, one on one, or even one against two, but since he lost, there had to be more than two. Two to hold him, while one knifed him, and for what?"

Clancy replied, "The way I see it, it was a senseless killin'."

Seamus, then asked, "Could it have been a mistaken identity? I mean with this country gettin' up in arms over this threat of civil war, could be he was thought to be, a spy if you will."

Clancy said, "I refuse to believe it was for a bucket of beer. That would make it more senseless than what I thought it was."

Flynn replied, "That would be a stretch too far, I believe. No, Lads, it wasn't for the beer, nor was it for a mistake in identity. This, I think, was pure, outright murder for pleasure. That is how I see this."

Clancy, then said, "Then, if that be the case," He spit in the palm of his hand, then got into a boxing stance saying, "it'll be a pleasure to extract a tooth for a tooth when we find out who done this terrible thing. Why, when I get my hands on them…"

Flynn said, "Easy there, Slumgullion. Tis not likely that will happen. In a township as large as Waco, I believe we will be chasin' shadows. Lengthening shadows that hide in corners, or in this case, hide in plain sight."

Seamus, then asked, "So, what do you think we should do 'bout Casey's death, Flynn Darlin'?"

Flynn replied, "Keep our eyes, and ears open for Timothy, and Kevin, and of course for anything that leads us to Casey's killers."

Seamus, then said, "Aye, that would the way of it, and logical as well."

Clancy said, "Look at him just layin' there so peaceful. I swear, he looks like he's just fallen asleep."

Flynn replied, "He *has* fallen asleep. He's in that forever sleep. And, why wouldn't he look peaceful? He no longer has the cares of this world to weigh him down, and then kick him when he is. I just hope he's in a far, far better place than the one he recently left behind."

Seamus said, "Aye. T'would be a great comfort to know that."

Clancy replied, "One can only hope." Pointing up, he said, "Well, you know."

Flynn replied, "That's where I was referrin' to, Clancy."

Seamus, then said, "The Lord giveth, and the Lord taketh away, and it doesn't matter how it's done."

"Aye." Flynn replied. "As the sayin' goes, only the good die young."

Clancy asked, "Makes me wonder just how old you have to be, to be good enough to die young?"

Flynn chuckled, then said, "That's one question I don't want to hear the answer to. I don't know 'bout you Lads, but it's time for me to go. Sorry Casey, but life must go on."

Seamus replied, "Aye. It does, but yes, it's time to leave."

As the men left the room where Casey lay on a table covered with a sheet, Ben entered the anteroom. The men themselves walked into the anteroom, preparing to leave the mortuary.

Ben asked, "Is there anything else I can do for you, Gentlemen?"

Flynn inhaled deeply, then exhaled, saying, "I'd say you've done enough, Sir. We thank you for all you've done so far."

Ben replied, "It's my business, Sir, and I'm very good at it, if I say so myself."

Flynn said, "I have no doubt, Sir. How much is the burial of our friend Casey?"

Ben replied quickly, "That would be ten dollars, Sir."

Clancy, then said, "That's a bit steep don't you think?"

With a twitch of his head, Ben replied, "Not from my point of view, Sir. It takes a lot to prepare a body for burial now days. No longer do we just dig a pit and drop the body in. I have done my best to accomplish that."

Seamus said, "I believe you outdid yourself, Sir."

Flynn dug in his pocket and came out with a $20.00 gold piece, then handed it to Ben.

Ben took the gold piece, then said, "Give me a minute, and I'll have your change."

Ben turned and left the room leaving the three men to watch after him.

Seamus, then said, "You don't need me to pay the man. I'll be outside gettin' some fresh air. The air in here is kind a stale, and musty."

Clancy said, "I'll go with you, Seamus. This place gives me the heebie-jeebies. The sooner I get out a here, the better."

Seamus and Clancy walked to the door. Seamus opened it, and stared wide-eyed at what he saw, then quickly shut it, turning his back to the door.

Flynn asked, "What's the matter, Seamus?"

Confused, Clancy, then said, "That's what I'd like to know."

Seamus stood with his back to the door looking rather disturbed about something.

Seamus replied, "You won't believe who I just saw with me own two eyes."

Muddled, Flynn said, "Well, tell us, man."

Seamus swallowed hard, and with eyes wide, he said, "Brass Tacks, and he ain't alone."

Flynn said, "Brass Tacks? Are ya sure, Fella?"

"As sure as I know me name is Seamus O'Neil, from Enniskillen, Ireland."

Flynn, then said, "May the sain'ts preserve us. How could he know where we are?"

Seamus replied, "The better question is, what do we do now? He is bound to find the wagon, and where the wagon is, we are."

Flynn, then said, "Tis true that. I never would have expected this turn of events. I need time to think. Let's get back to the wagon, quickly."

Before they could make their exit, Ben came back with Flynn's change from the $20.00 gold piece.

Ben handed the $10.00 silver coin to Flynn, saying, "Your change, Sir."

Flynn said, "Thank you." Then pocketed the silver coin.

Ben said, "It's goin' to be such a great funeral."

Flynn, then said, "I'm afraid our plans have changed, Sir."

Ben said, "They have?"

Flynn replied, "Yes, I'm afraid they have. We will not be able to attend the funeral of our dear friend, Casey O'Connor, as we had planned."

Ben said, "Oh?"

Flynn replied, "It's a complicated thing that must be dealt with immediately."

Ben answered, "That's too bad. Is there anything I can do?"

Seamus replied, "Thank you, no. It came up… quite suddenly."

Ben, then said, "I see. That's a shame. It'll be such a fine funeral. There will be no mourners to mourn the deceased, but that's quite alright. We'll get by."

Clancy said, "I'm sure you will."

Ben, then said, "Then, I'll be sayin' good day to you, Gentlemen."

Seamus brought the door ajar, peered out, then turned saying, "Good day to you, Sir." He turned to Flynn, and said, "Tis clear."

Then, both Flynn and Clancy turned to Ben, and said their goodbyes. The three, then left the funeral home.

It wasn't long until Slim returned to his family's private cemetery with shovels and a pick-axe he got from the barn. Slim handed Sheriff Mattew Tucker a square tip shovel to remove loose material, and the pick-axe to Ross. He kept the round nose shovel for digging.

Slim said, "Ross, break ground if you would. The sheriff and I will do what is needed until you need to break the ground again."

Ross began to break the ground for the burial plot. As they took the pick-axe, and the round nose shovel to dig the grave, the ground became harder. After the loose dirt, and earthly material was scooped up, and tossed away by Sheriff Tucker, the pick-axe was again used to break the ground.

Slim said, "I appreciate the help from the both a you. By myself it would take me a few hours to dig this grave."

Matt replied, "It's the least I can do for a good friend like your father was to me. He was a great man." Leaning on the pickaxe, he continued, "Of course, he was older than I, but for some reason, he took a great liking for me, even though at times, I was a klutz, and a stumble-bum. It was him who helped me become sheriff of Stephens County. Did you know that, Danny?"

Slim pushed his shovel into the ground for another shovel load, then replied, "Yeah, I knew that. He told me he was goin' to help you get elected. He did well."

Sheriff Tucker replied, "Thanks, Danny. I've done the best I could, but the way things have been," He sighs, then said, "I hate to say this, but I haven't done that good."

Slim replied, "There was no way you could control what was happening, Matt, so, don't blame yourself. You did what you could within the law. You couldn't prove anything Wade did, or what he had done was illegal. You tried, but there was only so much you could do."

Matt, then said, "He sure covered his tracks real well. Made everything he did look legal, at least on paper, that's for sure. No court would convict him."

Ross, then asked, "You couldn't find nothin' to arrest him for?"

Matt replied, "Not a thing. I probably could've, well maybe, got away with arresting him for tax evasion, but he'd probably slip by with only a slap on the wrist. Lack of evidence."

"But at least he would be in jail, wouldn't he?" Ross asked.

Matt answered, "Well, yeah, he'd be in jail, but what good would that do? He'd still be able to hand out orders even behind bars of a jail."

Ross, then asked, "What 'bout that hexagon bullet that killed your brother Randy? Ever find out who carries that rifle? What was it again?"

Slim said, "I haven't forgotten 'bout that bullet, but I haven't seen who uses it either. That rifle is a Whitworth Sniper Hexagon English-made percussion rifle. It's a .451 caliber, single shot muzzle loader. There were only a few of those made in 1857. A friend of mine at the time had one. It was very accurate, and has an excellent long range kill effect. Very spendy."

Ross asked, "And, just how far is that?"

Slim answered, "If I remember right,1,100 yards."

Ross, then said, "Wow, that's over one-third mile. That's quite a distance."

Matt said, "You wouldn't even hear the shot, and then you're dead, or wounded, and dyin'."

With Matt and Ross's help, digging Richard's grave took just a little over an hour to dig.

Then, Slim crawled out of the grave, and stood looking back at it. He then said, "I have a feelin' there'll be many more a those dug. Thousands even, once this civil war I been hearin' 'bout gets underway."

Matt said, "Some people claim that the south has a right to secede."

Slim replied, "As soon as get the election, we'll just see what rights the south thinks it has."

Ross, then said, "I'm not all too sure there will be a shootin' war. North against South."

Matt replied, "Southern states are seceding every month, or so I hear. I hear they already have an imaginary battle line separating the northern states, and the southern states. It's the Mason-Dixon line. It's the dividing line that was initiated in 1763, over an 80 yearlong land dispute. It seems appropriate."

Ross, then said, "Well, Danny, if the war does come west to Oklahoma, you goin' to stand with her if she does decide to secede?"

"I won't do that, Ross. I can't, and I won't. It goes against what I believe in."

Ross then asked, "You mean you'd fight against your own people? Most of them are your friends. Now, you know loyalties will be tested one way or another."

Slim answered, "I am aware of that, Ross, but if the south is intent on destroying the United States, and if my friends turns their backs on their own country, well then, they are no longer my people, nor are they any longer my friends."

Ross replied, "Those are strong words, Slim. I wonder if Mister Lincoln knows it could be illegal to stop the southern states from seceding."

Slim answered, "I wouldn't know. Question is, how would you know?"

Before Ross gave his answer, Matt said, "How 'bout we worry 'bout that when we have to decide."

Chapter Two

Quite Labor-Some

Slim said, "That decision could be made for us, Matt, but I do see your point. We have our own problem here to tackle. Devlin Wade."

Mat replied, "Yep. He's our shootin' war just now.

Ross replied, "That's true, but if Lincoln does get the election, the south will fight."

Slim, then said, "Well, no one elected Devlin Wade to where he is, and yet we're fightin' him, and his gunnies to keep what's ours. Some have given their very lives to keep him from getting what they have."

Matt replied, "Yes, they have, and now, they can no longer defend themselves, and they still lost everything they had to Devlin Wade."

Ross said, "I assume you mean to say, they died tryin'."

"That's exactly what I mean." Matt answered. "Could I prove Wade was behind it? No. Makes me sick to think he's gettin' away with it."

Ross then said, "That man is one dangerous human being."

With that said, all three men carried their tools back to the barn. When they then entered the bunk-house they found Mike Eagan laying on a bunk. With him was Victor Corman. The rest of the crew had gone to the herd, and their camp cook, Riley Crenshaw.

Slim asked, "Well, Mike, how you doin' this mornin'?"

Sounding a little disgusted, Mike answered, "Aw, I'm alright, Slim. A little stove up is all, and that's from lyin' 'round so dang much. Vic here won't let me move a muscle without givin' me some kind a tongue lashin'. Now, I ask you, is that any way to treat a friend for Pete's sake?"

Ross said, "It's for your own good, Mike. Don't be movin' 'round so much, or you'll cause that wound to open up again."

Mike replied, "Good Lord, how long does it take for that not to happen?"

Matt answered, "Quite a few days I'm afraid. It don't happen overnight, nor does it happen magically."

Mike replied, "Well, I sure am gittin' tired of it, that's for dang sure. I need to get up and do somethin'. Move 'round a little, ya know, but he won't let me. He's like some mother hen."

Slim chuckled, saying, "You need to stay where you are so that wound can heal. That's all you need to do. Comprende?"

Mike replied with a resounding, "Ye-e-es. You're just as bad as he is, you know that?"

Slim chuckled again, then said, "Wouldn't you be a little more comfortable in the house? We'd oblige you quick if you'd like."

Mike scoffed, then said, "Naw, I don't think so, Slim. I ain't fond a showing my weak, and weariness in front of a couple a women folks."

Ross, then said, "You don't? Even though they know you got shot? No shame in that,

is there?"

Sullenly, Mike replied, "Well, no, there's no shame in that. It's just… well, it just ain't a manly thing to do, is all."

Slim replied, "Alright, Mike, have it your way, but I still think you'd be better off in the house, but if you insist on stayin' in this rickety old bunkhouse, and lay on these flimsy clapboard beds, who am I to say no to that?"

Mike replied, "Flimsy? I'll have you know I have become quite comfortable on this clapboard bed, Slim. Only thing is, I need to get up and be 'bout so's I won't go stiff from not usin' the legs. You can understand that, can't you?"

Slim answered, "Yeah, I suppose I can. Non-use means no use. Nevertheless, only once, or twice a day, and with you holding onto something, or someone to keep from fallin'."

Mike replied, "Yes, Daddy. Did I say you're just like Vic here? Well, you are. Both a you, just like an ol' mother hen."

Victor chuckled saying, "The less you move 'bout the better, Mike. Things'll get better sooner than you think."

"Can't be soon enough for me, that's for dang sure." Mike replied as he turned to Victor, saying, "Mother."

Victor said, "Just listen to him, will ya? I just might thump him on the head for makin' that remark."

Recoiling, Mike, then said, "You wouldn't hit a man when he's down would you? And, an injured man at that."

Chuckling, Victor replied, "It'd make you forget 'bout your bullet wound."

Matt replied, I'll can assure you of that, Mike."

"Aww, I don't see that happenin' all too soon." Mike replied. "I've been boogered up before, but then, I've never been shot before." Scoffing, he added, "I tell ya, I'll be happy when this malady is over. This thing just lingers on like a rot gut whiskey hangover."

Slim said, "Well, if you don't stay still, and not move around so much, it'll take a whole lot longer to heal than you want it to."

Sighing, Mike, then said, "The sooner I'm done with this, the sooner I'll like it."

Matt said, "Sounds like you're a might brimful a nettle, Mike."

With a look of confusion, Mike asked, "Brimful of nettle? Could you put that in plain English, Sheriff? I don't know your meaning."

Matt replied, "You know what, "brim full', means, right?"

Mike answered, "Well, yeah. It means a cup, or glass, is full to over flowing the brim."

Matt, then said, "Correct. And, 'nettle', in this case, is an English term, which means you're irritated, aggravated, and annoyed with your current condition."

Mike looked at Matt with surprise, then said, "Wow. That's a mouthful of words."

Matt replied, "That was a bit wordy, wasn't it?"

"Have you two had breakfast?" Slim asked, as he changed the subject.

Victor replied, "Yes, we have. Jennifer made sure of that. Flap jacks and a ham steak."

Slim said, "Think I'll go in and refill my coffee cup."

Matt, then said, "Mind if I come with you, Danny?"

"I don't mind."

Ross also said, "Think I'll go in with you. I could use a cup a coffee myself."

Slim replied. "I believe we have enough ground coffee to usher in another pot of coffee."

As the three men left the bunkhouse headed for the main house, a rider came racing into the area. The rider reined his horse from a full gallop to a halt, and sat on a dancing horse. The horse was huffing, and puffing from being rode hard.

Eric Pendergast yelled out from the saddle, "Cattle rustlers! We believe them jaspers to be Wade's gunmen, but can't prove it."

Overhearing what Eric had said, Victor came running from the bunkhouse.

Victor, then asked, "Anybody hurt, Eric?"

"I'm afraid so, Vic. Greg Hickman, and Otis Ackerman. Greg's dead. I saw him fall just after the cattle stampeded. He didn't have a chance."

Slim asked, "And, Otis. Is he dead?"

"No, thank God." Eric answered. "He got away, but I could tell he was hurt."

Victor asked, "Did you see how bad he was hurt?"

Eric answered, "No, I didn't. I rode hard to get here to let you know what was goin' on."

Slim asked, "What 'bout the chuck wagon and Riley… what's his name?"

"Crenshaw? He's okay." Eric replied. "He made camp half a mile behind the herd, and thankfully for him they stampeded in the other direction."

Slim yelled as he turned, "Let's saddle up!"

Victor turned as he ran to the corral, "Eric? Stay here and watch over Mike."

Eric shouted back, "Watch over Mike? I'm ridin' with you after those cattle rustlers."

"Stay here. You got that?" Victor shouted back. "If we need you, we'll let you know."

As Victor cinched his saddle down, Eric dismounted asking, "Where is Mike? Main house, or bunk house?"

"Bunk house." Victor replied as he swung himself onto the saddle. "Keep him from movin' 'round so much, will you? We don't want that wound to open up again, and cause him more problems. Sorry, got to run."

As the four men kicked their horses in the flanks, and hurriedly rode away, Eric turned to go into the bunkhouse. In the bunkhouse, Eric found Mike lying on a bunk rack, resting on his elbow.

Mike asked, "What's this I hear? The cattle's been stampeded?"

"That's right. We believe it to be Wade's gunmen, but there's no way to prove it."

Mike swung his feet over onto the floor. He gave a moan of pain as he grabbed his wound.

Mike, then said, "I couldn't hear everything that was said, but did I hear you say that someone was hurt?"

"Yeah. Otis was hurt when we were attacked, but he got away."

"Damn! What else?"

"Greg was killed."

"He was murdered you mean!"

"Yeah, that's what I mean. After he was shot, he fell from his horse, and landed under the hooves of the stampeding cattle. Like I told Vic, he didn't have a chance. It was pure chaos. Guns blastin'. Men screaming, and yellin'. Cattle bawlin' as they went on the run."

"Anything else?'

"Not that I saw. 'Course, I nosed my pony towards the homestead, and rode hard to get here to let Slim know what was happening."

"How many you think jumped you?"

"Don't really know, Mike. It's hard to say. I could've counted one man three times, or more, that's how chaotic it was. But were I to guestimate, I'd say not less than 15."

"Meaning you were outnumbered."

"Most likely. They jumped us from out a nowhere. It happened so quickly. It took a minute, or better to react, it was that sudden."

"Is that when Greg was shot?"

"Yeah. He was shot when we were first attacked. I, then seen Otis get shot, but he was able to skedaddle, and get away. I dodged a few bullets myself. I was lucky to get away."

"So, you don't know what happened to the rest of the crew?"

"No, I don't. Like I said, I hightailed it, and rode hard to get here."

"I hope you did the right thing, Eric."

"I think so. What good would it had been if I had been shot, and killed like Greg?"

"I see your point. I hope they can turn the stampede, and get the cattle back."

"I just hope no one else gets killed doin' it."

With a painful groan, Mike swung his feet back onto the bunk, and laid his head on the pillow. Mike then said, "I sure made a mess a things, didn't I?"

As the four men came to where the cattle should have been, they noticed the gate and a few yards of fencing had been torn down, making it easy for the cattle to leave the pasture owned by Richard Siringo, now owned by his son, Danny Siringo, also known as Slim Siringo. A few hundred yards up, the grazing land they could see the chuckwagon, and a few horses. The horses were tethered Bermuda style. The men rode to where the chuckwagon was, then reined their horses to a halt. The men stepped down, and tethered their horses to the wagon wheel, and to the wagon tongue. Riley Crenshaw and the rest of the crew stood over the body of Greg Hickman.

Three other men were sporting some kind of bandages on their arms, or on their legs from wounds sustained during the cattle rustling, and stampeding cattle.

Slim, then asked, "Where are the cattle?"

Uriah replied, "Not far. We ran those jaspers off, but not before we tangled with them."

Solomon said, "We took the herd back, finally. They're a few miles from here."

Otis, then said, "They've settled down, and just millin' 'bout, so there's no threat of another stampede. They're just bawlin' 'bout their lot in life. Too tuckered out to trot."

Victor asked, "How bad you hurt, Otis?"

Standing with his left arm in a sling, Otis replied, "Nothin' broke. Bullet went clean through the upper arm. It does hurt a might for sure."

Victor looked at Uriah and Solomon, asking, "You two hurt bad?"

Uriah Spoke saying, "Naw. Just scratches and small cuts mostly. Nothin' serious. Just enough to irritate and aggravate the dickens out a you, is all."

Slim asked, "How many head a cattle did we lose? We had to lose a few."

Solomon replied, "We got lucky, Slim. We lost nary a one."

Slim smiled then said, "I like the sounds a that. None lost is a good day."

Riley spoke, saying, "No steer lost, but we did lose Greg Hickman."

Slim looked at Victor with eyes of compassion.

Victor said, "That's a tough thing to see. He was a good friend. He'll be missed."

Slim said, "Think of how they attacked you in town, and then you'll have a good idea on what they think of you, or any of us for that matter. Wade tries to take no prisoners if he can help it."

Matt, then said, "If he keeps killin' people off the way he's doin', he'll have no one left to steal from, or terrorize. A man like that needs those kind a people, or he'll wind up goin' insane with nothin' to do."

Scoffing, Matt replied, "Let's hope the latter happens first. Him goin' insane."

Victor, then said, "That would put a new wrinkle in this thing, wouldn't it?"

Slim said, "Yeah, but I believe it's a wrinkle everyone could live with. I know I could. He's been on us like a duck on a June bug."

Matt, then said, "And, baring his teeth like a dog gone mad with rabies. The only good thing to do when that happens is to put him out of our misery."

Ross, then asked, "Say, Slim, what happened to those three fellas you came in with. Walt, Fletcher, and Will. I haven't seen them around in quite a while. It seems odd."

Slim answered, "It does seem odd, don't it? I wonder just where they could be?"

Victor asked, "You don't suppose they had somethin' to do with this rustlin' business, do you?"

Slim turned to Victor, saying, "I highly doubt that, Vic. There's only one thing fellas like those three are good at, and rustlin' cattle ain't it."

Victor, then asked, "So, Slim, just where did you meet those three? Are they close friends, or just acquain'tances?"

"Jenny and I met them when we were on the westbound stage from Paris, Texas to Ringgold, Texas. We were on our way home to Comanche. Jenny found me in Paris when I was workin' on a cattle drive to Wichita, Kansas, tellin' me there was trouble here at home."

Victor, then said, "So, you became close friends on the stage?"

"Not really, no. They chased off an Apache war party that was attackin' us at one of the stage stops. There were six of them then, and, we called them the Ridge Riders, but to tell you the truth, they came here to work for Wade. Wade had sent for them, but when they met, things didn't work out so well. so when, they, and Wade had a falling out, they stayed on to lend a helpin' hand in gettin' rid of Wade."

Matt said, "They saved my hide."

Surprised, Victor asked, "How'd they do that?"

Slim replied, "A conversation overheard."

Matt replied, "Wade had already inserted his bought and paid for sheriff while I was in Duncan, the county seat, so, he had to get me out of the way. He set up an ambush to do just that when I was on my way back to Comanche. Those three met me on the road north of town. I thought I was bein' accosted, but when they told me what Wade had planned, I calmed down. Luckily for me they heard 'bout it, and put a stop to it. We rode to Richard's Homestead ranch."

Slim, then said, "Well, I have other things to worry 'bout, than to worry 'bout where those three got off to."

Uriah said, "You don't have to worry 'bout those rustlers, that's for certain. We shook 'em off like a bear with bees at a bee hive."

Solomon, then said, "That's right. They'll think twice before they tangle with us again. We put a hurt on 'em somethin' fierce."

Victor replied, "Yeah, maybe, but we paid a high price for that bit a hurt. Greg."

Slim asked, "He have any family?"

Victor replied, "None that I know of. He never spoke much of home, or family of any kind."

Uriah said, "He has a sister in Bluffton, Indiana. He told me so. Cynthia, I think he said."

Victor turned to Uriah, saying, "You got that much out a him, did ya?"

Uriah answered, "Slow night on night herd. He wanted to talk. He also said he has a younger brother livin' somewhere 'round Decatur, Illinois. Not sure where he said."

Victor, then asked, "He say what Cynthia's married name was?"

"Naw. He got quiet, then rode away." Uriah replied.

Riley, then spoke, "Well, gents, there's shovels in the flat box. May as well git a grave dug for him. I'll fashion a grave marker of some kind, to let folks know of his passin'."

Slim said, "Well, it's a cinch we can't go into town to the telegraph office."

There came a murmur of displeasure.

 Slim continued, "But if one is willin' to ride, he could head north to Duncan, and use the telegraph there. I think his family has the right to know what happened to him."

Matt said, "His sister is probably married with a couple kids, but who knows 'bout his brother? Last known where-abouts was somewhere near Decatur, Illinois. That's a poke and hope situation there."

Slim, then said, "Well, whoever decides to go to Duncan, send a telegram to Cynthia his sister."

Matt said, "Without knowin' what her married name is, let's just hope the right woman gets the message."

Ross said, "You boys take it easy. Looks like you need the rest seein' as how you're all boogered up the way you are. If Slim will help me, we'll dig Greg's grave."

Matt, then said, "It's only thirty to forty-five minutes to Duncan. I could stand by and wait for an answer from his sister if she does reply."

Slim turned to Matt asking, "So, does that mean you're volunteering' to go to Duncan?"

Matt replied, "I reckon so, Danny. Without realizing it, I suppose I did."

Slim said, "Well, you know the trail."

Matt replied, "I do, plus I know a couple short cuts to keep myself off the main road just in case Wade tries his luck again."

Slim said, "Good idea. He may have the main roads watched, but you keep your eyes, and ears open. Since your death didn't come 'bout the first time he tried for your demise, you can bet your bottom dollar he'll try again."

With that said, Matt untethered Shadow from the wagon tongue, then stepping into the stirrup, he swung himself onto the saddle.

As he reined Shadow away from the group of men, Matt breathed out, "Yeah." Then, as he kicked Shadow in the flanks, he clicked his tongue, then said, "Giddy-up, Shadow."

They, then galloped away from the group of men in a hurry.

As Matt rode away, Ross then said, "Break out the pick and shovel Riley. We have a grave to dig."

Riley turned back to the wagon, then reaching into the flat box he brought out a pick-axe, and a round nosed shovel built for digging.

Slim took hold of the pick-axe, and Ross took hold of the round nosed shovel.

They walked to a determined spot in the shade of a Blackjack Oak tree. There, they began to dig the grave. As Slim broke the ground, Ross pushed the round nosed shovel into the ground up to the hilt, grabbing a shovel load of dirt, then, chucked the load of dirt to one side. They wrapped the body of Greg Hickman in his bed blankets. Riley had fashioned making a grave marker using thick tree branches from the Blackjack Oak tree nearby. The vertical, upright branch was shaved to a point at the end to ensure penetration into the dirt. Then, when Greg was placed into the grave, and the grave had been filled in, Riley shoved the grave marker into the ground at the head of the grave to mark Greg's passing. Using the butt of his revolver, Riley drove the upright piece of the handmade wooden cross a little deeper into the ground. The men stood around the grave with their hats in their hands. They stood with morose, and sullen faces as Victor said a few kind words over the deceased. You could tell the words that were spoken were heart felt and sincere. It became clear that the men were anxious, and uncomfortable as they shifted from foot to foot. Then, the men slowly, but steadily turned, and stepped away from the graveside, going back to the camp area. From start to finish, the funeral of Greg Hickman took no more than ten minutes. Not one flower. Not anything. Just a few kind words said with a gentle, yet sad so long.

When Matt had gone a few miles from the grazing land of the Homestead Ranch, he topped out on a ridge. Reining his horse to a halt, he could see the main road from where he sat on Shadow. The main road lay below him less than a quarter mile away. Through the trees, he surveyed the main road to the north, then to the south, winding its way from Comanche about five miles to the south. He noticed nothing, or no one that would present any danger. Still, being careful, and wanting to stay off the main road to shy away from any trouble, he took to riding the ridge line that led to the north. The ridge line soon emptied out onto flat, open country in full view of the main road for about a quarter mile, or so. He rode at an easy lope through open country. The landscape was decorated with assorted foliage such as, the Homestead Verbena, creating clusters of rich colored flowers which were being assaulted by bees and butterflies. There was also Russian Sage, a silver leafed plant having blue upright blooms that smell like sage. Then, there were the Free flowering daisies of the Black-eyed Susan was spotted here and there with their colors ranging from yellow, to bronze, to mahogany. The ground cover was lush and green as he rode over the carpet of the, 'Indian Blanket', which created lovely red flowers tipped with yellow blooms, plus Burr, and Button Clover were scattered covering the ground. These were the last days of the month as May was giving way to the month of June.

He hadn't gone too far when he noticed a riderless horse standing alone munching on Burr and Button Clover near the mouth of a canyon known as Mulberry Canyon. Mulberry Canyon is not so deep as canyons go, but it isn't dry, not by a long shot. There are quite a few pools of water, and marshes located in Mulberry Canyon.

As he reined Shadow to a halt, he knew that this was not a good thing to find. He wondered what could have happened to the rider? Was the rider afoot looking for something? But as the horse moved around, he noticed an Indian arrow stuck in the saddle near the saddle horn. He quickly became alert. He surveyed the area all around himself for danger from those who disposed of the man who rode that saddle horse. Matt had a horrible feeling that the man was lying dead somewhere, or worse… wounded. Dead most definitely would be better than wounded and find himself in the hands of Indians, no matter what tribe it is. Wounded, the man would be taken prisoner, and later, the man would be tortured, then he would be killed just for sport by the young braves who had newly attained their adulthood. Killing that man would be a rite of passage, so to speak, for the young braves. Matt slowly rode across the expanse of space between him and the riderless horse. Ever alert, he kept his head moving from left to right while trying to keep the horse from galloping away. When he got within a few yards from the horse, he stepped down, and started to slowly walk toward the horse.

The horse snorted at Matt as it flapped its lips. It sighed, then ambled a few feet away, and again lowered its head, and began to graze on the clover. Matt had gotten close to where he could see the arrow sticking out from the saddle. From what he saw of the markings on the arrow, it was Comanche.

As he edged closer to the horse, Matt was softly saying, "Whoa, Son. Easy, fella. I ain't goin' to hurt you. Whoa, Boy."

Soon, he was close enough to see red stains on the right fender of the saddle. Dried blood. Then, the horse suddenly raised its head, looking to its left. Matt dropped to one knee, looking under the horse to know what the horse was looking at, or was hearing. He didn't know what the horse had heard, or what it had seen, but soon, he himself heard the pounding of horses' hooves as they came closer, his direction. No yelling, nor screaming of a warbling war cry, just the pounding of horses' hooves headed his way. He sprinted quickly from the kneeling position to Shadow. He quickly mounted, then kicked Shadow in the ribs. As they took off like the wind, he looked back to see the riderless horse whinny, then quickly run away in a westerly direction, away from the oncoming riders. He didn't know if it was Indian, or white man that spooked him and the horse. He wanted to avoid trouble at all costs from either one.

He had something much more important to do in Duncan, and he didn't have time to tangle with Indians, or white men looking to cause trouble for someone. If he had anything to say about it, nothing, or nobody was going to stop him from doing just what he intended to do in Duncan. He rode hard for the few miles that were left as he traveled the main road, then he entered Duncan. He rode to the telegraph office, stepped down, tethered Shadow to the hitching post, then entered the telegraph office. The telegrapher was elbows down on the counter, chin resting in the palms of his hands, and his eyelids stubbornly trying to stay open. As Matt swung the door closed behind him, the telegrapher knee jerked himself to come to somewhat awake.

Matt then said, "Wouldn't it be a whole lot more comfortable to be sittin' in the chair when you fall asleep?"

The telegrapher replied, "Sorry, Sheriff. It's just been one of those days. It's been quite labor-some to stay awake today for some reason."

Matt chuckled, then said, "I've had days like that myself, Earl. Danged if I know the reason why either."

Earl yawned, then asked, "What can I do for you, Sheriff?"

Matt answered, "I have a telegram to send."

Earl replied, "I figured as such." Reaching under the counter, Earl brought out a piece of paper and pencil. Wetting the tip of the pencil on his tongue, he said, "Okay, Sheriff, what's the message?"

Matt relayed the message for Greg Hickman's sister Cynthia in Blufton, Indiana.

Earl wrote the message down, then said, "That will be a dollar and two bits, Sheriff. Is this county business?"

Matt replied, "No, it isn't, Earl. It's personal. This comes out of my pocket."

Earl brought out a money box from the shelf under the counter, and put the money Matt handed to him in the box, then put the money box back on the shelf under the counter. He, then asked, "Where will you be, Sheriff, should there be a return message?"

"Hopefully I'll be at Reggie, and Mary Carver's. She's expecting to give birth just 'bout anytime now. I'm beginning to think she's awfully selfish in not wanting to share that beautiful life inside her to the world." Expecting, yet not getting a reply, Matt, then said, "Anyways, that's where you should find me should there be a return message."

Earl said, "Alright, Sheriff. I'll get this off right away."

At that point, Earl sat down in the chair at the table where the telegraph key was, and he began to tap the key to open the line. As Earl began to send the telegram, Matt turned, leaving the telegraph office. He mounted Shadow and reined him toward the Carver house that lay 50 yards east of town, just off the eastern main road. It was the only house within a hundred yards of the place. When Matt rode up to the house, a buggy was parked out front. He realized the rig must belong to Doctor Doug Beecher, MD out of Duncan. Doc Beecher must've come out to assist with Mary's delivery of her overdue baby. Matt was told the last time he was in town that Mary Carver was overdue by a few weeks. Both Mary and Doc Beecher was concerned.

Paul Stroud, and Karl Stokes, was ordered by Devlin Wade to pay a friendly visit to the Silver Shovel Silver Mine, southeast of Comanche by a few miles. The reason? To let the two men, Amos Stegner, and Seth Brubaker know they are on private property while working a silver mine allegedly belonging to Wade. And, especially to keep the profits from that illegal work. When they arrived and halted their horses near the opening shaft of the mine, there was no one around. They looked around the area, but found no one. Did the two leave? Were the two captured and taken prisoner by Indians? Was there a cave-in somewhere deep inside the mine? They didn't have long to wait for an answer to those questions. One man working a wheelbarrow came from the main shaft of the mine. The man was dirty, covered in dust. He was wearing a miner's hat with a miner's head lamp. He wore a dirty, dingy yellow shirt, and tan to brown trousers, scuffed up, high laced boots. When he saw Paul, and Karl, he sat the wheelbarrow down where he was. He breathed heavily, then, he spat dirt from his mouth. He took his kerchief from around his neck, shook the dust from it, then wiped his face to remove some of the dirt from around his eyes and from off his face. As he retied the kerchief back around his neck, he looked at the two men with assumption and mistrust. He grabbed a canteen that was nearby, pulled the cork, and took a mouthful of water.

He rinsed his mouth with it, then spit it out. He, then took another mouthful of water, and swallowed it. The man wiped his mouth with his dirty shirt sleeve, then said, "Ah, there's nothin' like the taste of cool water, is there?" Getting no reply, he then asked, "What can I do for you fellas?"

Karl replied, "It'd be more like what we can do for you and your partner, Seth Brubaker."

The miner recorked the canteen, then asked, "Oh? How's that?"

Paul, then said, "We're here to give you some real good advice, Amos."

Amos looked at the two men befuddled, then asked, "Just how is it you know my name, yet I don't know yours?"

Karl replied, "Our names are not important. It's the name of the one who sent us to deliver a message. That name is important."

Amos replied, "Uh, huh. I suppose I can guess what that name is, can't I?"

Karl chuckled, then said, "I believe everyone knows what name that is, Mister Stegner."

Amos, then asked, "Okay, what's the message?"

Paul replied, "You are hereby warned to cease, and desist working of the silver mine, that is not your silver mine, and keeping the profits of said silver mine, that is not your silver mine by order of Devlin Wade, said owner of the Silver Shovel Silver Mine."

Amos turned to Paul saying, "He said a lot, to say so little."

Paul smiled, then said, "I believe he got the message across."

Amos replied, "True. I couldn't help but figure out what that message was, even after his long proclamation. Out of curiosity, I wonder what would happen if we were to turn down that offer to just pack up and leave?"

"Dire consequences, I'm afraid." Paul replied. "If you know what I mean."

Amos answered, "I do indeed. You say Devlin Wade owns this silver mine?"

Paul replied, "He does, and he gives you just 24 hours to be out a here."

Amos, then said, "He does?"

Paul replied, "24 hours is all he gives you to be gone."

Amos, the asked, "And, he has the proof of ownership?"

Karl replied, "I assume he does, yes, or we wouldn't be here."

Amos, then replied, "Uh, huh."

Amos looked around while he rubbed his chin as in thought. Then, he noticed his partner, Seth Brubaker, hiding aside a boulder just up the hill, and behind them, looking down the barrel of a Henry rifle, giving him cover.

Amos, then said, "Well, you fellas just tell Wade the answer is no. It will always be no from now till doomsday. We'll have to be carried out a here feet first, or buried here."

Paul replied, "That can be arranged, Mister, but we'll tell him what you said. He'll be entertained with the thought of having you buried here, but we'll tell him. We'll tell him."

Amos, then said, "I expect you fellas should be moseyin' along now. Have a safe trip back to town, and have a good day."

Paul and Karl mounted their horses, and reined them back towards Comanche.

Seth came bounding down the hill to where Amos was, asking, "What was that all 'bout, Amos? Who were they, and what did they want?"

Amos answered, "They was hired guns of Devlin Wade. They was tellin' me that Wade owned this mine, and we was warned to pack up and leave."

Seth swore, "Why, them no account claim jumpers. If I'd a know'd that, I'd a plugged 'em both."

Amos said, "Yep, and you'd be on the run for murder for the rest a your born days, too."

When Paul and Karl returned to Comanche, they tethered their horses to the hitching rail in front of the saloon. They, then went inside, then to Wade's office. They knocked on the door.

Wade said, "Come in."

When the office door opened, Wade looked up at the two men with speculation. Then, the door latched as it was closed.

Wade, then said, "What did Amos Stegner, or Seth Brubaker, say when you explained to them that they were on private... my property? And, did you tell them it was illegal to work a silver mine that was not theirs, and keep the profits of that mine?"

Paul replied, "Oh, you know, Boss, the same old song and dance. You know the tune. Me and Karl told him they have 24 hours to pack up what's theirs and leave, or there would be harsh consequences. More to the point… dire consequences."

Chapter Three

Contact At Waco

Wade smiled happily, then said, "Good. Good. We'll give them 24 hours, and if they're not gone in that amount a time, we'll bury 'em."

Paul chuckled, then said, "I told Amos that what he said would greatly entertain you."

Wade looked at Paul, smiled, then asked, "Well? What did he say?"

Paul replied, "Speakin' of bein' buried, he said when it came to them leavin', the answer is no from now till doomsday. He, then said that they'll either be carried out a there feet first, or they would be buried there."

Wade gave a look of befuddlement, then asked, "He say that?"

Paul answered, "Yep, as sure as you're born, Wade. Ask Karl. We both heard him swear to it. Kind a spunky 'bout it, too, if ya was to ask me."

Wade rose from his chair, and went to the window. He stared out of the window for a few seconds, then, his facial expression changed. His lips spread a little. His eyes widened, realizing that that statement not only entertained him, but it also amused him.

He smiled a feral smile as he turned back to Paul saying, "You're quite right, Paul. That does entertain me. Yes, Sir. It entertains me quite well, Quite well indeed."

Karl asked, "Is there something else, Wade?"

At the window, Wade replied, "No, I'm very much amused, and entertained now. That statement made my day. It'll take a lot to take that feelin' away from me." He turned to both men saying, "There's nothin' else, Gentlemen. Go, and enjoy yourselves."

As Wade continued to glare out of the window, he heard the door latch closed. He turned from the window to find himself alone. Out in the saloon itself, Paul, and Karl bellied up to the bar.

Paul slapped his hand down on the bar saying, "Give me a whiskey, Fred. It's time to howl at the moon."

Karl yelped, "Make mine a double, Fred. I'm with Paul here. It's time to pain't the town."

Fred asked, "What color, Karl? Red, or blue?"

Karl replied, "Red, of course. I'm way too happy to pain't the town blue. Matter a fact, give me a bottle of your finest whiskey, and a glass."

Fred, then said, "And, what of you, Paul? You know what it means to howl at the moon?"

Paul answered, "Yep. You have certain thoughts you wish you never had, and you don't understand why you have them. I'll take a bottle myself, Fred. I have thoughts I don't quite understand."

Fred scoffed, then said, "You two are quite the congenial types today, ain't ya?"

Karl paid no mind to what Fred had said, but Paul? He took real offence to it. Paul reached across the bar, and grabbed Fred by the shirt front causing Fred to drop the glass of whiskey.

As Paul pulled Fred toward him, Paul said, "You cussin' me, Fred? Callin' me that congengy, congangy, or whatever you said, 'cause if you are…"

Mumbling incoherently, and very much afraid, Fred replied, "You mean congenial?"

Paul said, "Yeah. That congengy-thing."

With eyes wide and a terror stricken face, Fred said, "That word just means friendly. Honest, that's all it m-m-means. I s-s-swear."

With that said, Paul released Fred's shirt front. Fred staggered back away from the bar with a wistful look. Paul turned to go grab a table, then turned back to Fred, eyeing him cautiously.

 Paul, then said, "If I find out different Fred, friend, or no friend, I'll put a bullet in you, and I'll` feed your eyes to the hogs, and your tongue to the wolves."

Fred swallowed hard, then said, "I s-s-swear, Paul. It means friendly. H-honest."

Paul reached and grabbed his bottle of whiskey from the bar, causing Fred to have a knee jerk reaction to it, and he backed away, encompassing half the length of the bar with fear on his face.

In the hotel hallway, Lieutenant Lundstrom hollered, "Sergeant Ashburn?"

Master Sergeant Roy Ashburn rounded a corner in the hotel hallway.

He answered, "Yes, Sir?"

"Has everyone had breakfast, Sergeant?"

"Yes, Sir. Early."

"Good. We should be leavin' Whitesboro within hour, Sergeant. Make sure every trooper is aware of our departure."

"Yes, Sir. Any special orders, Sir?"

"Special orders? No, no special orders."

"Very well, Sir. Will the doctor sign the release for the wounded, Sir."

"With, or without that release, Sergeant, these troopers are goin' back to Fort Richardson for proper medical attention."

"Yes, Sir. I take it you don't care for this civilian doctor. Doctor Crittenden?"

"No, Sergeant, I don't. He angers me. He's unrestrained in his thinking."

Confused, Sergeant Ashburn asked, "How's that, Sir?"

"He thinks his Hippocratic Oath has a far greater weight than that of the US Army."

"I beg the lieutenant's pardon, but what I see is his concern for, and the welfare of his patients, Sir. Military, or civilian. After all, he is a medical doctor, and he has his duty to perform, Sir."

"Well, Sergeant, everyone has their own opinions. I also have my duty to perform, and the fact still remains, those troopers are leaving Whitesboro today. Signed release, or not."

"Yes, Sir."

"Ready the troop, Sergeant."

"Yes, Sir."

Master Sergeant Roy Ashburn turned on his heels, and walked the hallway until he got to the stairway going down to the foyer, and the main lobby of the hotel.

During that time, Lieutenant Lundstrom had gone into Jamie's room. When the lieutenant entered the room, where he was met by Doctor Larry Crittenden. The doctor was making his rounds for the diagnosis of his patients, tending to their wounds, and their availability to be moved. The lieutenant stood idly by waiting to hear Doctor Crittenden's diagnosis of 2nd Lieutenant, Jamie Carlson's wound. Doc Crittenden inspected Jamie's head wound, whereupon he took the wound cream, and reapplied the cream to Jamie's wound.

As he rewrapped Jamie's head with a clean bandage, Doc said, "This is comin' along just fine, Jamie. You'll be good as new in a few days. I see no reason why you can't go to back to Fort Richardson with the lieutenant here."

Jamie replied, "Thanks, Doc. I must admit there isn't much pain at all now. And, my vision has returned to almost normal."

Doc, then said, "Well, now, that is good to hear. It'll get better as the days go by."

Lieutenant Lundstrom reacted negatively when he heard that information. He then said, "You had partial vision, Lieutenant, and you said nothin' 'bout that?"

Jamie answered, "I'm sure I mentioned it, Lieutenant. If I didn't, I apologize for that oversight, Sir."

Lieutenant Lundstrom replied, "I'll dismiss it for now, Lieutenant, but it will go down in my report."

Jamie said, "That's fine, Lieutenant. I've already put it down in mine."

"You had partial vision, and yet, still, you were able to write a report, Lieutenant?"

"No, Sir. I could not. Sergeant Major Dickerson, wrote down my report when I asked him to write it down for me."

Lieutenant Lundstrom replied, "I must admit, Lieutenant, that was good thinking. Tryin' to remember what happened from memory in your condition, tid-bits of information could be unnoticed, and very important facts and details could be lost. I'll take your report, Sir, and turn it in to Colonel Mackenzie with my report when we arrive Fort Richardson."

Jamie replied, "I appreciate the thought, Lieutenant, but I will hand in my report to Colonel Mackenzie myself. I am not finished with my report. There are still additions to be made."

Lieutenant Lundstrom, then said, "And, if I were to order you to do so, Lieutenant, would you still refuse to obey that order?"

"Yes Sir. There is no reason for you to make such an order. I am in charge of my report until I hand it in to Colonel Mackenzie at Fort Richardson."

Lieutenant Lundstrom then said, "Very well, Lieutenant. That will also go down in my report. Your refusal to follow an order from a Senior Line officer."

"As you wish, Lieutenant." Jamie replied. "But you actually never gave me that order. That was just a query as to what I would do if you were to give me that order."

"You worded that well, Lieutenant. I will not give that order. After all, as you said, that order would be unwarranted. But I suggest you make yourself ready to depart Whitesboro in 45 minutes."

Jamie replied, "Yes, Sir. I will be ready to leave as soon as Doc Crittenden here gives his say so."

Lieutenant Lundstrom then said, "Doctor Crittenden has already given his say so, Lieutenant, saying you were able to travel. Is there anyone else you need to see, Doctor?"

Doc Crittenden replied, "No, Lieutenant, there is no one else. I have given my medical diagnosis for every trooper who came into my care, and to be honest, they are all able to travel, though precautions must be made, and adhered to."

Lieutenant Lundstrom then said, "I have a physician's assistant with me for such a task, Doctor Give him the precautions if you would. I am satisfied that all is at the ready, Lieutenant."

"As am I, Lieutenant." Answered Jamie.

Doc Crittenden stood saying, "Well, Jamie, since you are able to travel, I wish you the best. Also, I will sign the release paper, if that suits you, Lieutenant Lundstrom?"

"That signing of a release paper was your idea Doctor. Not mine."

"That, Lieutenant is my insurance if anything was to go wrong on your trip home."

"And, you call me self-centered."

Opening his black bag, Doc Crittenden said, "I have the release paper here dissolving my affiliation to these troopers, having their names affixed, and their medical care given over to the medical aide provided by Lieutenant Lundstrom of the US Cavalry on this date. With my signature and his, it will relinquish my relationship. I will advise Eli Harris, the hotel owner."

Doc Crittenden and Lieutenant Lundstrom both signed the release paper. Lieutenant Lundstrom, then said, "This release paper is a waste of time, Doctor."

Doc Crittenden, replied, "To you, yes, but for myself, I relinquish all medical care to the US Cavalry, and have no more say as to their care. That signed paper says so."

Doc then folded the sheet of paper, and handed it to Lieutenant Lundstrom.

Doc Crittenden, then asked, "Well, that's out of the way, Lieutenant. Tell me who and where I might find your physician's assistant, Sir."

"I will send him to see you Doctor. 2nd Lieutenant, Adam Murtaugh is knowledgeable of such things, and he is a welcomed addition to the Cavalry."

Doc Crittenden looked at Lieutenant Lundstrom a little mystified.

"Do I detect a slight appreciation for the medical profession from you now, Lieutenant?"

Lieutenant Lundstrom gave a leering look at Doc Crittenden, then said, "I had a moment of weakness, Doctor. I'll try not to let that happen again."

Doc Crittenden smiled at Lieutenant Lundstrom, then turned to Jamie saying, "Have a safe trip, Jamie."

Jamie smiled, then replied, "Thanks, Doc."

Doc Crittenden stepped to the door, opened it, then turned back to Lieutenant Lundstrom.

Doc chuckled, then turned, closing the door behind him. Lieutenant Lundstrom stood staring at the closed door. He, then shook as if he suddenly had a cold chill.

He said, "I detest that man. He gets under my skin more than any man I've ever known. Other men have done the same, but that man is the worst of the many." He turned to Jamie, saying, "Signing that release form was a waste of time. With or without that release, you and the others are leaving Whitesboro, Lieutenant… today."

Jamie replied, "I'll inform the others of our departure. The only thing I need to know is when that time is."

Lieutenant Lundstrom said, "Hopefully, no more than an hour. By then, it is my hope that Whitesboro will be just a memory."

Jamie, then said, "A very good memory I might add, Lieutenant. At least I think so. No matter what you think of Doc Crittenden, he pulled us through our dilemma good and proper."

Lieutenant Lundstrom replied, "I never said he wasn't a good physician, Lieutenant. The man himself is who I don't like." Scoffing,he added, "He just rubs me the wrong way. Well, I better have Lieutenant Murtaugh go see Doc Crittenden, or we'll never get out of here."

Jamie rose from the bed where he was sitting and followed Lieutenant Lundstrom out of the room, then closed the door behind him. Lieutenant Lundstrom went one way down the hallway toward the staircase, while Jamie went the other direction. Jamie was going to inform the men of the detail of their departure, and to be ready to leave, hopefully within the hour, per Lieutenant Lundstrom's orders. Lieutenant Lundstrom went down the staircase, and then out of the hotel. He went to the wagon where 2nd Lieutenant, Adam Murtaugh, Corporal, Frank Sande, and Private, Spencer Ellsworth was making room in the wagon for the detail to be taken back to Fort Richardson under medical care. Lieutenant Lundstrom stood at the rear of the wagon looking into the rear of it watching the effort to make room in it.

Lieutenant Lundstrom said, "I suppose I need to go to the saloon to find Sergeant Major, Del Dickerson, and Scout, Ned Grayson, so listen up. We should be moving out in less than an hour, I hope, but still be ready."

Lieutenant Murtaugh, then said, "All right, Lieutenant. We'll be ready."

Lieutenant Lundstrom said, "Lieutenant Murtaugh, you are to go to see Doctor Crittenden so he can give you the precautions he has for the wounded."

Lieutenant Murtaugh came to the rear of the wagon and looked down on Lieutenant Lundstrom.

"I am well aware of the precautions for the wounded, Lieutenant. I don't need to…"

"That is an order, Lieutenant." Lieutenant Lundstrom replied. "I will not be held up a minute more because of an oversight. Is that clear, Lieutenant?"

"It is, Sir."

"Good." Lieutenant Lundstrom replied. "Make it quick, will you?"

Lieutenant Murtaugh then asked, "Is he in the hotel, or his office?"

"Last I saw, he was in the hotel."

"Just my luck I'll have to go lookin' for him." Scoffed Lieutenant Murtaugh.

"Then do it, Lieutenant, find him and do it quickly. Time is of the essence."

Lieutenant Lundstrom, turned on his heels and headed for the saloon to find Sergeant Major, Del Dickerson, and Army Scout, Ned Grayson to inform them of their departure. When he got there, he stopped at the saloon doors and looked into the saloon. He saw Ned Grayson at a table off to his left with his head down on it. The lieutenant sighed heavily knowing that Ned Grayson was dead drunk. He did not see Sergeant Major Del Dickerson in the saloon, but he had a good idea where he could be. He entered the saloon, stopped, and noticed the stairs leading to the second floor. He turned to look at the bartender with a questionable look. The bartender knew the look, so he held up three fingers indicating room three. The lieutenant tapped the brim of his hat with his finger, indicating a 'Thank you'. The bartender acknowledged the thank you with a head nod. The lieutenant, then climbed the stairs to the second floor. He didn't need to look for room three. There was enough noise coming from the room that it was evident where it was. The lieutenant stopped in front of room three which had the number three nailed to the door. There came a lot of laughter and giggling coming from room three. He grabbed hold of the doorknob, and quickly entered the room. There, in bed with a blonde-haired woman, was Sergeant Major, Del Dickerson. Both were nearly in the buff, and was completely surprised, and off guard when the lieutenant rushed into the room unannounced.

The blonde-haired woman had the look of distress on her face as she began to desperately, and hurriedly cover her breasts with the sheet. Sergeant Major Dickerson had the look of complete disbelief on his face as Lieutenant Lundstrom stood in the frame of the open door. The Sergeant Major sat up on the bed with a look of surprise realizing who it was.

Lieutenant Lundstrom, then said, "Sergeant Major, you have less than an hour to be ready to leave Whitesboro. I do hope you will be available for that departure. We will leave with, or without you Sergeant, going back to Fort Richardson."

Sergeant Dickerson replied, "I'll be ready, Sir. Thank you, Sir."

Lieutenant Lundstrom smiled saying, "Excuse the interruption, Ma'am." He winked, then said, "Carry on, Sergeant."

Sergeant Dickerson smiled back saying, "Thanks, Lieutenant."

As Lieutenant Lundstrom left room three, he closed the door, then headed for the stairs. As he went down the stairs, he knew Ned Grayson would be a handful to remove from the saloon. He left the saloon and headed for the wagon. There he found Corporal, Frank Sande, and Private, Spencer Ellsworth sitting on the wagon box. Sergeant Everett Sutrell had gone with 2nd Lieutenant, Adam Murtaugh to find Doctor Larry Crittenden.

Lieutenant Lundstrom, then said, "Scout, Ned Grayson is in the saloon with his head down on a table. The man is obviously dead drunk. You two go carry Grayson here to the wagon and make him comfortable. If, and when he does wake up, fill him full of water."

Corporal Sande, then said, "Water, Lieutenant?"

The lieutenant answered, "Yes, water."

The corporal replied, "Water would just keep him on a continual drunk, Lieutenant. That means he would stay drunk dang near until we got to Fort Richardson, Sir."

The lieutenant answered, "Exactly, Corporal. Just what I'm hoping for."

Flynn McDonagh, Seamus O'Neil, and Clancy Burrows had left McQue's Mortuary in a hurry after viewing the body of their friend Casey O'Connor. He had been stabbed and killed on his way back to the Etsy barn from the Buckhorn Saloon. Seamus had just seen Brass Tacks and a group of his men enter Waco, Texas looking for the wagon of weapons. The three men quickly went to the Etsy barn where the weapons wagon was located. They were unsure of what to do next. They had not yet met Flynn's contacts, Timothy McFadden, and Kevin Taylor, to transfer the weapons wagon to them. The sooner, the better. Knowing that Brass Tacks, or one of his gunmen, would eventually find the weapons wagon, caused them a great deal of anxiety. After making a quick inventory of the boxes of rifles, and making sure none of the boxes had not been pilfered through, and none of the rifles had been stolen, Flynn sighed a heavy sigh of relief knowing that that was not the case. He sat down on one of the boxes breathing a little heavy, a little out of breath. They say worry will make you look old, or is it make you feel old? Both maybe. It can cause high blood pressure. Fatigue, both physical, and mental. It will also cause tension, that brings about irritability. Make a person lash out at someone, even a friend, for no reason. Whatever it does to a person, all three men happened to display one, or all of those symptoms pertaining to too much worry brought on by anxiety.

Seamus, then said, "We need to move the wagon."

Clancy replied, "I agree, but where? We were lucky to find this spot."

Flynn said, "Aye, we were. Give me a few minutes, Lads. I need time to think."

Seamus said, "I'm not sure how much time we do have, Flynn Darlin'. They can spread out like a spider web, and find the wagon in no time a'tall."

Flynn answered, "I'm well aware of that fact, Seamus. Just, just give me a few minutes, will you? I need to come up with a plan."

Seamus, then said, "That would be a great idea, Squire Darlin'."

The three men, then quieted down allowing Flynn to come up with a plan to foil Brass Tacks attempt to find the weapons wagon, and possibly shooting them just for the fun of it.

Clancy, then said, "I know this may sound crazy, especially with what's goin' on here, but I'm hungry. We have yet to eat today."

Flynn turned to Clancy, saying, "With the trouble we're in, I hadn't even thought of eating. Strange how that is."

Seamus scrunched up his face, then said, "I wasn't hungry until you mentioned it. Now, I could eat a Banger and Mash with an Irish Red to wash it down."

Flynn's face softened as he said, "Not I, Lad. A bowl of Irish Stew would do me kindly, with sliced pan, and a Murphy's Stout to wash it down."

With sparkling eyes, Seamus replied, "Either, or, would be just grand."

Clancy said, "Me, I'd like to have steak and eggs with biscuits and sausage gravy with a pot a coffee. Maybe even a ham steak and eggs. My stomach thinks my throats cut."

Seamus, then said, "Now, that does sound quite good in and of itself, doesn't it?"

Clancy remarked, "My throat bein' cut?"

Flynn replied, "No, Clancy, your breakfast menu."

It took but a second, or two after what he just said for Flynn's face to have that sullen look again. His cheery mood also withered away. His mindset was attuned to the problem they find themselves in. They had to have a plan to escape the harsh consequences if they were caught by

Brass Tacks, and his gang of outlaws. The idea of that happening did not sit well with either of the three men, and they verily expressed their displeasure of it.

Flynn, then said, "It doesn't matter what plan I come up with, we can do nothing without the horses hooked to the wagon, and ready to roll, so let's get that done."

Seamus smiled, and said, "Sounds like you're formulatin' a plan, Squire Darlin'."

Flynn replied, "Let's just say, I'm workin' on it, Seamus. I'm workin' on it."

The three men went to the corral and began to put the harnesses and rig on the team of horses, then hooked the team to the wagon.

Seamus, then asked, "And, Flynn Lad, what plan have you come up with?" He turned to Clancy saying, "I bet it's a good plan too."

Clancy smiled, then replied, "I bet it is too. I can't wait to know what it is."

Flynn said, "So would I, Lads. So would I."

Both Seamus, and Clancy turned to Flynn with eyes wide, and a confused look on their faces.

In jumbled terms, Seamus then said, "Tis not the time to be jokin' 'round, Flynn. Do you not know how much trouble we're in ever since Brass Tacks rode into town? Surely you have a plan to escape with these guns, as well as, with our lives." He waited for a reaction, but got none, so he went on, "I'm kind a fond of who I am. I've known me all my life, so, please tell me you have a grand plan to avoid having to suffer such indignation."

"As I said, I'm workin' on it."

Clancy then said, "I stand with Semus, Flynn. I'd like to see the sun go down tonight, and then see its rise tomorrow. Since those men rode into town, I haven't got that guarantee, aside from interference of providence."

Flynn remarked, "Let's get on board, and we'll take the wagon to a dry wash I saw just outside of town on our way in. That way we can keep our eyes on these guns, and Brass Tacks won't be snoopin' around out there."

Seamus, then said, "If it's the same dry wash I seen, ain't that too far out? Tim, and Kevin won't know where we are, and these guns will never be transferred."

Flynn climbed aboard the wagon, and while sitting in the box, he said, "We'll cover the wagon with tree branches and shrubbery. A disguise to keep interested parties from finding these guns."

Clancy said, "You must mean those lyin', stealin', back-stabbin', mean, no good, lowdown, no accounts, Brass Tacks, and his gang a hired thugs?"

Flynn replied, "Tis exactly who I mean, Clancy." He smiled.

Clancy and Seamus then climbed aboard the wagon, but just as Flynn picked up the reins to the team, a voice cut through the air causing a great pleasure to cross Flynn's face. The voice yelled Flynn's name.

With a face full of surprise, Flynn hollered, "I'd know that voice anywhere! Delira, and excira, if it isn't Timothy McFadden!"

Seamus yelled out in surprised recognition, "And, Kevin Taylor!"

Timothy McFadden, and Kevin Taylor stood out in front of the team of horses.

Smiling wide, Tim hollered back, "And, just where is it you was goin', Flynn Darlin'?"

Flynn jumped down from the wagon seat, and with a sheen of happiness that glowed like yellow gold across his face, and a smile from ear to ear, he and Tim grabbed hands, and shook hands vigorously. He, then took Kevin's hand, and gave a vigorous handshake. Seamus, then followed suit. The four men were almost as giddy as a school boy at this reunion. Clancy stood idly by while this friendly reunion took place, and reveled in the joy of his companions.

After the pleasantries were taken care of, Flynn asked, "Now, how did you know we were here, and how did you know where we were?"

Tim answered, "We went to the Buckhorn saloon and talked to Burl, he owns the saloon. He said there were some Irishmen askin' if we knew where to find us, me, and Kevin."

Excitedly, Kevin, then said, "And, we were told that there was a chance you were here at the Etsy barn, so, we took a chance, and sure, and by gosh, here ya are."

Tim was looking around the barn, then asked, "Where's me Cara, Casey? He off chasin' the ladies, is he?"

Flynn and Seamus became morose, and glum. They looked at each other with sad eyes.

Kevin looked confused, then said, "What's the matter, Lads? You two look like you lost your best friend."

Seamus replied, "As a matter of fact, Kevin, we did."

Timothy turned his head to look at Flynn out of his peripherals saying "And, what did ya mean by that, Flynn?"

Flynn cleared his throat, then said, "There's no good way to say this, so I'll come right out with it."

Kevin asked, "Just what is it you're tryin' to tell us, Lad?"

Flynn looked at Seamus, then turned back to Timothy and Kevin saying, "Casey is dead. He's laid out over at McQue's Mortuary. We were just over there payin' our last respects, and sayin' our last goodbyes."

The look on both Tim, and Kevin's faces was complete and utter surprise.

Tim asked, "My God, Man. What happened?"

Seamus replied, "From what we understand, Casey was comin' back from the Buckhorn saloon with a bucket of beer for me, when he was assaulted and pulled into an alley by a gang of cutthroats intent on robbery, and then Casey was knifed to death. The constable here has yet to find the culprits what did the dirty deed."

His face full of unbelief, Kevin, then said, "That's terrible news, Flynn."

Flynn breathed deep, then said, "I know. But we have bigger troubles than that."

Tim said, "Oh? And, that is?"

Seamus replied, "These guns."

Kevin said, "Now, why would this wagon cause folks to wonder what's on it, when there are other wagons here the same size, and what looks like to be the same cargo?"

Clancy, then said, "Trust me, it has caused quite a commotion when we got here."

Tim stepped over to Clancy, turned to look at Flynn, then turned back to Clancy, saying,

"And, just who might you be, Lad?"

Flynn replied, "His name is Clancy Burrows, He volunteered to fight our cause in Ireland, so he'll be goin' with you, and these weapons to Matagorda on the coast. He's a good man, and he's been a great help these last few days he's been with us."

Kevin smiled wide, then said, "Well, now, that is good news. I bid you welcome, Mister Burrows."

Clancy smiled, then said, "Clancy will do, and it has been a pleasure, so far anyway. Until today."

Tim turned to Flynn asking, "What's wrong with today?"

Clancy replied instead, "You ever hear of a man they call Brass Tacks?"

Tim turned back to Clancy saying, "I have. So, what has he got to do with this?"

Flynn answered, "We bought these weapons off of him a few days ago, and on that same day, he sent his men to get them back by stealin' them back, and killin' us."

Kevin said, "I've noticed, happily I might add, they didn't succeed."

Seamus replied, "No, Jaysus, they didn't, but this very day, he, with the rest of his men, rode into Waco." He scoffed, then added, "How he knew where we are, I haven't a clue."

Tim said, "He must have eyes everywhere, so, how 'bout we get this wagon out a here, and on its way to Matagorda. There are three horses at the Livery waitin' for ya. They've been paid for, so just tell the proprietor your names, and you'll be on your way. Unfortunately, there is one too many horses now that Casey is no longer with us."

Seamus asked, "And, just where is the Livery? We could switch from Casey to Clancy."

"You passed it on the way in, I believe." Kevin answered. "At the edge of town."

Tim, then said, "We'll take the wagon and go to a dry wash behind the Etsy barn 'bout a quarter mile amongst a Pecan orchard." He turned to Clancy saying, "We'll wait for you there."

Flynn replied, "We'll be there, Tim."

Tim asked, "I thought you had other plans, and you needed to leave right away?"

Flynn answered, "I do, but it can wait. It isn't every day we four get to chat."

Kevin replied, "Tis true, tis true. It has been some time since we've had a chance to chat, hasn't it?"

Tim, then said, "How 'bout we have our little chat out at the Pecan orchard? Tis a bit safer there, I think."

Flynn replied, "Aye, it would be, wouldn't it? We'll be out there as soon as we can."

With that said, Flynn, Seamus, and Clancy left the barn going to the Livery stable to collect

the horses already paid for by Tim. At that same time, Timothy McFadden, and Kevin Taylor

had climbed on board the wagon, and was moving the wagon to the designated spot by the Pecan orchard that had just been discussed. The only sound was the creaking, and the groaning of the wagon, and the slap of the reins over the horses' backs, plus Tim yelling at the horses to move.

When they reached the Livery, Flynn asked the owner, Phineas Deeb, for the horses already bought and paid for on reserve for them.

Phineas replied, "Be glad to gents, Phineas Deeb at your service. One horse had a loose shoe, so, I had him taken over to Kurt Lattimer for reshoein'. He's our Farrier ya see."

Flynn asked, "I see. Just how long before he's returned do ya suppose?"

Phineas replied, "Aw, it shouldn't take too long, 'course it does depend on what he's workin' on now, and how many are ahead a ya."

Clancy then said, "Why don't you two go ahead on. I'll wait here for that other horse and I'll be along directly?"

Phineas walked over to his desk and picked up a piece of paper. He turned to Flynn, Seamus, and Clancy. He then asked, "Let's see here now. There's a Flynn McDonagh, a Seamus O'Neil, and then, there's a Casey O'Connor on reserve. Would you be those three Gentlemen?"

Seamus replied, "Aye, we would be, except for Casey. He was killed last night."

Phineas queried saying, "I'm sorry to hear that. You're not from 'round here, are ya?"

Annoyed, Clancy remarked, "No, we're not from 'round here."

Taken aback, Phineas said, "My goodness, Mister. No need to chew my head off."

Clancy, then replied, "Sorry, Mister, but we're just gettin' tired of havin' to hear people ask that question."

Phineas answered, "I can understand that, but it ain't often," clearing his throat, "we have Gentlemen, such as yourselves, come to..." clearing his throat, "yes, well..." He turned his gaze back to the piece of paper, saying, "Now, Gentlemen, the Livery bill. In the last three days..."

Flynn, then asked, "The bill wasn't taken care of?"

Phineas replied, "No, Sir. That McFadden fella, I think his name was, he said you fellas would be comin' into Waco in the next two, three days, and the livery bill you'd be payin'."

Seamus replied, "That was right nice of ol' Timmy, wasn't it?"

Flynn,then said, "Aye, but he did buy the horses. However much that came to."

Clancy asked, "Just how much did you sell those horses for?"

Phineas rubbed his chin in thought, then said, "I believe I sold those horses to your friends for $20.00 apiece. Yes, Sir, $20.00 apiece. Made a nice profit."

Clancy replied, "I just bet you did. Let's see the horses you have."

Phineas, then said, "Bout this bill…"

Clancy said, "Let's see the horses first."

Phineas replied, "Certainly. Right this way, Gentlemen."

When they left the Livery office, they walked the breezeway between stalls that were occupied, and those that were empty. Half way up the breezeway, Phineas stopped.

Turning to his right, Phineas, then said, "This horse, and the one to the left are two of the horses I sold to your friends. As I said, the third horse is at the Farriers for a loose shoe."

Clancy said, "I'll check them over, if you don't mind."

Phineas shrugged his shoulders, saying, "Makes me no never mind. Their yours anyways, so go ahead on. Check all ya want. You'll find the saddle, blanket, bridle, and bit there."

Chapter Four

Strange Times

Clancy took the bit, and bridle, then attached it to the horse. He opened the gate and led the horse out into the breezeway. While Clancy checked out the horse, Flynn and Seamus stood idly by waiting to hear his opinion on the condition of the horse.

Phineas shook his head in disgust, then said, "I assure you, Gentlemen, that that horse, and the other one are in fine shape, and in good condition, other than the one with the loose shoe, that is. He shouldn't be too much longer, I expect."

Clancy, then said, "This horse is as Mister Deeb said he was. He's in fine shape, and in good condition."

Phineas said, jubilantly, "See there? I told you, didn't I? When it comes to horses I don't lie. Not nary a word a lie."

Flynn then said, "As to the Livery bill, just how much would that be, Mister Deeb?"

Phineas brought the piece of paper up to read the amount listed, then said, "For three horses at a dollar a day, for three days? That would be nine dollars. Now, as for the feed. Three horses at a rate of fifty cents per day? That comes to 'round a dollar and fifty cents, times three, equals four dollars and fifty cents. Your total is fourteen dollars and fifty cents, Gentlemen, payable for the Livery bill. Also, you need to pay the Farrier for the loose shoe."

Seamus then asked, "And, we'll know how much that is when he returns with the shoed horse?"

Phineas breathed out, "Most likely, yes. Normally, it's a dollar for the reshoein' of a horse, in case you're wonderin.'"

Flynn shook his head, saying, "This has been a most rewardable, and profitable day for you, Sir. Hasn't it?"

"I can't deny that, but it's just business, mind you."

Flynn replied, "Yes, quite."

Phineas asked, "You fellas been in the states long?"

Seamus replied, "Quite some time now. Why?"

"Just wonderin' if you think we'll get into a shootin' war like everbody thinks we will?"

Flynn replied, "Oh, I don't think so. At least, I hope not."

Phineas, then said, "Things can't get any worse than some folks tellin' other folks how to live and what to do in their life. Makes me so dadblamed mad when folks do that. I figure them folks has enough problems in their own life without makin' trouble for other folks. Don't quite understand why they do that. I really can't."

Flynn asked, "Is that so?"

Phineas, then said, "Sure, that's so. It seems they're in an all fired hurry to start this shootin' war over the most pitiful thing ever there was. Somethin' called, states' rights. Ever heard of it?"

Trying not to further fuel the fires of Phineas Deeb's questions on the expectation of a shooting war in the United States, Flynn made his answer short and to the point.

Flynn replied, "No, I haven't, Mister Deeb. No, I haven't. Nor do I care to. T'would be a great disaster, and terrible thing when folks, such as myself, who work hard every day to scratch out a livin', then, to make it that much harder to do so in the near future just to stay alive."

Phineas, then said, "I can see where that could work against you, yes. Then, will you be leavin' the states should that happen, goin' back to wherever you're from?"

Flynn asked, "To Ireland? No, I believe we'll still be here to see it happen if it does."

Phineas, then asked, "Ireland you said?"

Flynn replied, "Aye. Tis Ireland. Been gone too long."

Seamus replied, "Aye, that we have. Far too long."

As Clancy grabbed the saddle blanket and saddle. Phineas grabbed the bit and bridle, put them on the horse led him from the stall.

Phineas, then grabbed the saddle blanket and saddle, threw them on the horse, and cinched the saddle down.

Phineas tethered the horse to the stalls top rail, then said, "The bill for the Livery if you don't mind, Gentlemen."

Flynn reached into his jacket pocket for his elongated leather wallet saying, "Of course."

Handing Phineas fifteen dollars, Flynn said, "Keep the change."

Phineas replied, "I thank you."

Just then, Kurt Lattimer was seen coming towards the Livery leading the horse by a rope.

Phineas, then said, "That wasn't long, Gentlemen. Not long a'tall."

Kurt replied in his Swedish accent, "I got on this right a away, Phineas. He's a real fine horse here, whoever he belongs to. He's in fine condition, except for that loose shoe, but I took care a that, and I inspected the other shoes as well, and I found them in good shape."

Clancy then asked, "That's kind a you, Sir. How much for the shoe?"

Kurt answered, "That'll be a dollar, thank you."

Again, Flynn took a dollar the wallet and handed it to Kurt.

Kurt replied, "I thank you kindly. Thank you."

As Kurt was leaving the Livery, Phineas went and grabbed the bit, and bridle, the saddle blanket, and the saddle. He carried the saddle gear to the horse that Kurt had just delivered. He, then proceeded to saddle the horse.

When Phineas had saddled the horse, he turned saying, "I appreciate your business, Gentlemen."

Clancy, then said, "You're welcome, Mister Deeb. Well. it seems we're ready to go."

All three men then mounted their horses. Said their goodbye's, and rode away toward the Pecan orchard, and the wagon of weapons.

And, of course there was their friends, Timothy McFadden, and Kevin Taylor. It has been quite some time since they had the chance to get together and talk amongst themselves. It would be such a joy to do that without the threat of any trouble, or having to keep looking over their shoulders. Clancy was quite captivated with these two Irishmen, Timoth McFadden, and Kevin Taylor. He was very much impressed with their attention to details, and the length they would take to complete their mission. They were, as Flynn and Seamus have been, ever aware of what could happen next, and the way to avoid it, if possible. The only thing he could say about the friends he has recently attained is they are like minded, and loyal to their country, as they should be.

Sheriff Tucker knocked on the front door of the Carver home. The door was opened by Reggie in less than a minute. Reggie invited Matt into his home.

Concerned, Matt asked, "How's Mary?"

Nervous and pacing back and forth, Reggie said, "I don't know, Matt. Doc's been with her for quite a while now. I haven't heard a thing. It's been awfully quiet in there."

Matt, then said, "Well, Reggie, I'm sure everything's okay. I think Doc Beecher has everything under control in there. So, there's nothin' to worry 'bout. Is there?"

"Lord knows, I hope not." Reggie replied, as he wrung his hands. "I'm wearin' out the rug with my pacin' back and forth. I may need to replace it."

Matt forced a chuckle, then said, "I just might join you. I hope your rug holds up."

"Hmph." Reggie replied as he paced. "Right now, I could give a rats…"

Just then, they heard a slap, and then a baby's cry. They looked at each other smiling.

Matt took hold of Reggie's hand and shook it vigorously, saying, "Congratulations Reginald. You're a father of a?" He turned towards the bedroom door, then said, "Well, I figure we'll know the answer to that question any time now."

Reggie was grinning like a bird fed cat, repeating, "Yeah. Yeah." Matt chuckled while Reggie kept repeating, "Yeah, yeah."

A short time later, Doc Beecher opened the door and walked into the living room wiping his hands with a cotton rag.

Reggie rushed over to Doc asking, "Well, Doc? How's Mary, and the baby?'

Doc Beecher replied, "Both are doin' just fine, Reggie." He turned back to the door, then back to Reggie saying, "That was the best quill baby birth I ever had the pleasure in bein' a part of."

Reggie turned to look at Matt who stared back at him, both befuddled.

Reggie turned back to Doc Beecher asking, "Quill baby? I'm afeared I don't know what you mean there, Doc."

Matt, then asked, "Yeah, Doc. I ain't never heard of a quill baby myself. Oh, I think I know what that means."

Reggie turned to Matt asking, "Yeah?"

"Yeah." Matt answered. "That means that the baby is a boy because he has a, well, you know. A quill."

Reggie turned from Matt saying, "That's the funniest name for…"

"And, he'd be wrong, Reggie." Doc Beecher replied.

Reggie became exasperated, then said, "Well, what is a quill baby, Doc?"

Doc said, "I'll explain that after you go see your wife and son."

Reggie had a knee jerk reaction, then yelled out, "A son! I have a son!"

As Reggie went in to see his wife, Mary, and his new born baby boy, Doc explained to Matt what a quill baby was. Matt listened intently, then laughed when Doc got to the end of the explanation.

Matt, then said, "I can't wait to see Reggie's face when you tell him what a quill baby is. Talk 'bout a shocker?"

Doc tossed the cotton rag down in the waste basket that was near an end table. He, again, went in to pick up his black bag, and instruments. Reggie was so dadblamed proud of having a son, he pranced around like a proud peacock while holding his son. Doc saw the joy, and the smile on Mary's face, he smiled with her.

As he gathered his instruments, Doc said, "Don't drop him, Reggie. He just breathed his first breath of air."

Reggie replied, "Aw, Doc, I ain't goin' to drop him. You never did say what a quill baby was, so, what's a quill baby, Doc?"

Doc looked over at Mary who was smiling at him from under her covers on the bed.

Doc smiled, then said, "Reggie, quill baby is just that, a quill baby. That's when a woman who is in labor, but cannot bear down because of lack of strength to build enough pressure for delivery, a quill is used with a little snuff in the quill."

Surprised, Reggie said, "Snuff? In the quill? But Doc, I don't dip snuff."

Doc replied, "I happen to carry snuff, and a quill in my bag for this very reason. It doesn't take much, but the doctor will blow a dab of snuff from the quill into the nose of the woman causing the woman to have a sneeze reflex. In other words, an, ACHOO!, which causes the woman to build enough pressure in the diaphragm to deliver a baby without any harm to the mother. Of course, she might have the temptation to dip snuff from here on." Doc turned to Mary and winked at her saying, "I suggest you not do that nasty habit, Mary. Gum disease is nothing to sneeze at."

Mary replied in a weary, squeaky voice, "Yuck, Doc. That I can promise."

Doc straightened himself then said, "Two of the most beautiful things in the world is a new born baby, and the glow of a mother who just delivered that baby."

Mary, then said, "Aw, Doc, I don't glow."

Doc replied, "There's a glow 'round you, Mary, like the glow 'round a full moon. It's warm, and gentle, and I am amazed whenever I am a part of the birthing event. One dies, and another's born." He cleared his throat, then said, "I think they call that, the circle of life, Reggie. Quite remarkable, and miraculous as well, if you was to ask me."

Reggie, then said, "I'll tell you what a miracle is, Doc. Me, having a son."

Doc picked up his black bag, then turned to Mary saying, "I'll be back in a day, or two,

Mary, to check up on you and the baby. Hopefully, by that time you'll have a name for him. It'd be kind of odd not to have one."

Mary chuckled, then replied, "I think that can be arranged, Doc."

Reggie turned to Doc saying, "That's a sure thing, Doc." Reggie turned to Mary, who nodded her head, and smiled. Then, Reggie turned back to Doc Beecher saying, "His name will be inscribed in our bible as, Douglas, Matthew, Carver."

Doc Beecher replied, "Well, I'll be doggone. That's fine of you, folks. Mighty fine. I thank you both kindly."

Reggie, then said, "When you leave, Doc, could you send Matt in? I'll let him know he's a godfather."

Doc replied, "He'll be surprised, but I'll let him know you want to see him."

Still amazed, Reggie, then said, "Thanks, Doc."

Mary, then asked, "You think he'll be surprised, Reg?"

Reggie replied, "He'll be ecstatic, Mary."

The baby began to fuss a bit, so he gave Douglas, Matthew, Carver, over to Mary.

Mary, then said, "He needs to be fed, Reg. I don't think Matt should be in here when I feed little Dougie."

At the mention of his name, Reggie stiffened his back, and strutted like a proud Peacock

to the door. When he opened the door, he came face to face with Matt, who was trying to enter the bedroom, so, Reggie ushered Matt back into the living room.

Looking a little miffed at not being able to see the boy, Matt, then said, "Say. What is this? Can't I even get a peek at the little feller, Reggie?"

Reggie answered, "You'll have to wait awhile, Matt."

Matt replied, "Oh. They're both asleep, are they?"

Reggie chuckled, then said, "No, but Mary is feedin' the boy. I don't think…"

Matt shook his head as he replied, "Oh, no, no. Of course not. That wouldn't be decent."

Reggie, then said, "We decided to name the boy after Doc Beecher, and gave him his first name as, Douglas."

Matt smiled saying, "That's swell of you. I bet Doc was surprised."

"Yes, he was. Mary and I want you to be Doug's godfather, as well as..."

Matt stammered a bit, then said, "Me? A godfather? Why, I can't…."

Reggie butted in saying, "I expect you'll have to, Matt."

Confused, Matt asked, "I'll have to? Not that I mind, but why would I have to?"

"Because his middle name is, Matthew. Your name. Douglas Matthew Carver."

Matt stood stunned for a second, then said, "Matthew? Why saddle him with that name?"

Reggie was taken aback by Matt's reaction, so, he took a step back, and stared at Matt in unbelief.

Reggie, then said, "Hey, now, here I thought you'd be more than happy 'bout this, Matt. Why, I even told Mary you'd be ecstatic. But this is how you react?"

Matt reached out and took hold of Reggie's right hand and shook it vigorously. Reggie stared at Matt befuddled as they shook hands.

Matt, then said, "I am ecstatic, you dope. I just didn't want him to be saddled with my name, 'cause it hasn't' done so well with me, you know. But I'm as giddy as a school boy."

Reggie's demeanor changed at that as he smiled from ear to ear.

Reggie said, "You had me worried for a minute, Matt."

Matt, then said, "I didn't think my reaction would make you angry, but it did."

Reggie replied, "I must admit, I was gettin' a little hot under the collar."

Matt, then said, "Well, I hope you've calmed down now, because I sure do thank you, and Mary, for doin' this. I'm as happy as a pig who found a puddle."

Smiling, Regie replied, "Well, that's better. Good. Let me check on Mary right quick. She might be finished feedin' little Dougie."

Matt said, "I take it was Mary who called him, little Dougie?'

Reggie stared at Matt saying, "Yeah, she did You want to tell her not to?'

Matt took a step back, shaking his head saying, "Who? Me? Not me! I may be dumb, but I ain't stupid." He scoffed saying, "Little Dougie it is. For now, anyways."

Then, Reggie opened the bedroom door, and disappeared inside closing the door behind him. Matt wanted to go in, but then again, he didn't, because of the delicate nature of the moment. Matt took a step back as he listened to the murmured voices inside the bedroom. He strained to not only hear, but also to know what was being said. Matt was beginning to feel anxious, and a bit awkward as he shifted from one foot to the other. Then, Reggie again, appeared in the door way. He, then stood back with the door ajar, then he fully opened the door. Matt stood still, unmoving as he looked at Reggie with speculation shone plainly on his face.

Reggie, then smiled saying, "Go on. Go on, Matt. Go see your godchild."

Concerned, Matt asked, "And, Mary?"

Reggie smiled from ear to ear, then said, "Oh, good Lord. Will you get in here?"

Matt went to the door, stepped into the doorway, then peeked around the door frame. He seen Mary smiling back at him. She looked so peaceful, and beautiful even with her hair a mess. He turned to Reggie and smiled. He, then stepped into the room. Reggie walked around

Matt, and Matt took a step back thinking he was in the way as he watched Reggie go to the bedside away from him.

Mary, then said, "Hello, Matt."

Caringly, Matt replied, "Hello, Mary."

Mary, then said, "Come closer, Matt, and see your godson."

Mary unwrapped the cover from little Dougie's face so that Matt could see him. Matt stepped to the side of the bed and was straining to see little Dougie.

Mary chuckled, then said, "Oh, for goodness sake, Matt. Come to the other side so you can see him a lot better."

Matt straightened, then replied, "Well."

Matt walked to the other side of the bed.

Matt looked at Reggie, then, turned to look down on the angelic face of his godson, Douglas Matthew Carver. With what little hair the boy had was all mussed because of his covering. Douglas, then yawned, stretched a little, and scrunched up his nose. That caused Matt to.

Matt said, "Oh, Mary. He is just so beautiful, and so small."

Reggie laughed and said, "Well, yeah, Matt. You wouldn't expect him to be born as a teenager would ya?"

Matt quickly turned to Reggie, laughed saying, "Aw, no. That would never work."

Mary, then asked, enthusiastically, "You want to hold him, Matt?"

Matt took a step back, turned to Reggie who just smiled at him.

He turned back to Mary saying, "Who? Me? Hold the baby? No, aw, I don't think so, Mary. He's so small and so… small. I might drop him, or hurt him in some way, so no, I, I, I."

Mary asked, "You sure? He's light as a feather."

Matt replied, cautiously, "I'd bet the feather outweighs him." Matt began to sidestep along the edge of the bed, saying, "Well, folks, I 'spect I best be goin'. Thanks again for makin' me his.. godfather 'n all. I sure appreciate that." As he rounded the foot of the bed, he said, "Well, it sure was nice seein' you again. I'll come back by sometime in the next few days." When Matt came to the door, he opened it, then said, "Well, see ya."

The door closed behind him and latched.

Confused, Reggie stared at the closed door saying, "See. I told you he'd be ecstatic."

Then, the front door opened and latched when it closed.

Mary replied, "More like scared to death, if you ask me. Poor thing."

Reggie chuckled then said, "I wonder if he took his horse?"

As the wagons hurried along, Captain Gary Locke rode to the head of the wagons, and sat his horse just off to the side of the trail.

Captain Locke began hollering, "Let's move along, Men. We need to be back at the fort in no time."

As the wagons rolled past him, Captain Locke removed his cover, and began waving it in the air in a forward motion. Presently, 1st Lieutenant, Micah Chapman reined in beside Captain Locke.

Lieutenant Chapman, then asked, "You have the same gut feelin' I do, Captain. We haven't seen the last of those Indians, whether they be Kiowa, or Comanche, or whoever."

Silence for a second, or two, then, Captain Locke said, pessimistically, "I have that feelin' of bein' watched, Lieutenant. Problem is, who's watchin'?"

Lieutenant Chapman replied, "I like to know that myself, Sir, but I do know what you mean. I have that itch at the back of my neck somethin' fierce."

Captain Locke, then said, "Be aware, Lieutenant. Keep your eyes, and ears open for any kind of trouble. We're not out of this mess yet."

"Yes, Sir." Lieutenant Chapman replied, "I'll be one happy man when we get back behind the walls of Fort Richardson."

Captain Locke, then said, "Take the column, Lieutenant."

"Yes, Sir."

At that, 1st Lieutenant, Micah Chapman rode to the front of the column.

Then, Captain Locke hollered, "1st Sergeant? Send out two gallopers to Colonel McKenzie requesting support troops for the column. Explain why. You got that, 1st Sergeant?"

"Yes, Sir." Turning in his saddle, 1st Sergeant, Gene Ralston hollered, "Privates, Streat, and McCracken. Front and center!"

Both men jumped their horses out of line, and in quick time, joined Captain Locke where he was sitting.

When both men reined in beside the captain, the captain, then said, "You'll be gallopers to Fort Richardson and Colonel McKenzie. Tell him we have been under attack by the Kiowa. Send support troops for the column, asap. Streat, you leave now."

Private, Carl Streat replied, "Yes, Sir."

Private, Carl Streat suddenly bolted away from the column at full gallop, and sped away from the column towards Fort Richardson.

Captain Locke hollered after Private Streat, "Good luck, Private! And, hurry up every chance you get" He turned to the other private saying, "McCracken? Wait five minutes and then, you take off."

Private, Hugh McCracken replied, "Yes, Sir."

Captain Locke, then said, "You'll find your place near the front of the column, Private. When you've reached five minutes, be on your way, and, good luck to you."

Private McCracken replied, "Thank you, Sir."

At that said, Private McCracken rode near the front of the column, and edged his way into place.

Captain Locke rode to the front of the column, then looked back at Private McCracken.

Captain Locke, then said, "You keep accurate count, Private. You hear me?"

"Yes, Sir."

Captain Locke said, "You heard what I called out to Streat as he left, right?"

Private McCracken replied, "Yes, Sir. Hurry every chance you get."

Captain Locke answered, "Good." He scoffed, then said, "You'll make corporal in nine, or ten years."

Amongst the guffaws, and laughter from the troop, Private Hugh McCracken replied, "Thank you, Sir."

1st Lieutenant, Micah Chapman said, "That brought out the beast in these men, Captain."

Captain Locke turned to 1st Lieutenant Chapman and smiled, Then, both men chuckled.

As the five wagons of dead and wounded men alike rattled on, five minutes had passed, and without so much as a how do you do, Private McCracken suddenly broke from the ranks, and took off at full gallop in the direction of Fort Richardson. And, as sudden as his break away was, there arose from the troopers in the column, cheers of encouragement and glee.

Captain Locke removed his cover, waved it in the air saying, "Git' er done, Boy."

Then, the shouts and cheers of Private McCracken's break away died down after a few seconds, down to a low hum of extended grunts, and groans that mingled with the sound of the wagon wheels ever moving, and creaking over worn-out wagon tracks. With the excitement settling down to a ne'er do well, here comes the Jud-bub drudgery of keeping your distance, and keeping your cadence with a cadence call, called, 'Old Lady'. The song is a traditional work song, and it was ordered by Captain Locke to enhance morale amongst the troops. And, yet, there you are under the hot sun, and it blazing down on you like hot grease. And, not only that, the constant jarring, bumping, and being bounced around from side to side either by the horse, or the wagon you're on as it is being jerked from one side to the other by the lay of the land. Deep ruts, high ground, and mounds of dirt, not to mention the large rocks coming up against the wheels. After a while in the hot sun, each man had to put their bandanas around their faces to cover their noses due to the rotting corpses in the wagons. The aroma was hideous, and retching, and caused a few men to empty their stomachs by heaving their guts. The aroma was beginning to gag the wagon drivers, so much so, they traded places with mounted trooper so the wagon driver could escape the aroma that permeated the wagon. Every trooper knew it was a pitiful situation for the wounded in those wagons because there was no escape for them. The aroma was ever present, and it caused each trooper to vomit. Captain Locke reined in beside Lieutenant Chapman at the front of the wagons after riding the line of wagons for a loose wheel, or any other problems. He saw the Lieutenant wiping his face with his bandana.

Captain Locke, then asked, "Too hot for you, Lieutenant?"

"Some, Captain." Lieutenant Chapman replied.

Captain Locke said, "This Texas heat takes some gettin' used to, and the only way to get used to it is to be out in it."

Lieutenant Chapman again wiped the sweat from his brow, then said, "I transferred here from Fort Meyer, Virginia, six months ago, Captain, and I'm still not used to this heat. I swear I have sweat comin' out of every part of my body. I believe I have become one large sweat gland, Captain."

Captain Locke chuckled, then said, "It takes a while, Lieutenant, but you'll get used to it, or at least you'll be able to tolerate it like I do, but I must admit it does have its moments."

Lieutenant Chapman said, "It drains your strength, Sir, as well you know. The heat makes a man feel weak, and it's hard to regain their strength."

Captain Locke replied, "Plenty of water, Lieutenant. Plenty of water whenever possible."

"Yes, Sir."

"Keep yourself hydrated, Lieutenant, as much as you can."

And so, as the day wore on, the wagons rolled on. The sound of horses' footfalls, metal ring against metal. Horses whinny, or troopers cough. The creaking, and moaning of the wood of the wagons under a heavy load. The birds in the trees got quiet when the troop got close. Each man in his own thoughts, and they were thinking these were strange times to be in the Army. Each man had to come to terms with himself. He had to know where his loyalties lie when, and if, a shooting war should happen. The troopers looked around at the other troopers realizing that the friend they now have may become their enemy tomorrow. There were southern troopers on this detail, as well as, northern troopers. It became quite evident the war drum would sound, and the nation would be at war. It didn't matter that Lincoln, and other moderates had no intention of trying to destroy slavery, especially where it was already established. And, as strange as it was, the southern defenders of slavery could, or would not accept the idea that the institution of slavery was wrong. The way a southerner thought, especially when it came to slavery that if a man stands against slavery it was a slap in the face to a southern gentleman. If Abraham Lincoln won the election to the presidency, the south swore to destroy the union, and they would keep their institution of slavery. The Constitution bound all states together by mutual consent. That consent was being withdrawn by a few southern states. Captain Locke knew that if a shooting war started while he was on this detail, he would have no control over those in his command. Their loyalty would be somewhere else. He was almost certain he would be firing at his own men. That thought made him sick to his stomach. The thought also unnerved him to even think about. Captain Locke, then thought, '1st Lieutenant Micah Chapman came from where? Virginia? That made him a southerner if that be true. Drawing a bead on him staring down the barrel of a Remington Army revolver was just disgusting. He was a damn good officer. Would he want to be discharged after his return to Fort Richarson? Hopefully, he would not find the answer to that question, at least until his return to the fort, if a shooting war was to start'.

Selling guns to the Indians was no longer as profitable as it once was, but every now and then, it did become the thing to do when the money flow became slow, or nonexistent. They took to selling guns and ammunition to whoever paid the highest price. Loyal to nothing, and loyal to no one. Those who made their money in that kind of trade was loyal to only one thing, and that was the filthy lucre gotten by selling those items to the highest bidder, be it Indians, or northern, or southern states. Those who were for the south out west began giving guns to the Indians after obtaining their word to help them fight for the south should civil war break out. Those gun deliveries had to be stopped, and quickly. The south needed money, and fast in order to support the war. Gold was needed from California, and from Colorado, and silver from the Nevada silver mines. From large to small towns all over the west who had a newspaper, they all carried in printed word, the possibility of a civil war. Even the printed handbills that were being passed from pillar to post, they even embellished the inevitable possibility with facts and figures. Even word of mouth from one man to another caused more trouble than the written word in some cases. The telegraph sent the word all over the country through their wires, thus creating a volatile situation that could easily explode like sticks of dynamite at any time, and at any place throughout the west, and that included, Comanche, Oklahoma, Stephens County. Ever since the telegraph was invented by Samuel Morse in 1837, it has carried the news, good, bad, or indifferent, over the wires installed in towns of American citizens all through the west. If a shooting war does break out, the telegraph will, undoubtedly, carry that news far and wide much to the dismay of many citizens. It may even become a vital instrument in supplying information of troop movements, as well the sad news of the mounting dead on both sides… should the shooting war ever happen. Hopefully, it won't, but one can never tell when the death of an idea becomes reality on the docket in the court of inquiry in the minds of men. Captain Locke shuddered to think that a few men were intently thinking of an actual shooting war.

Captain Locke and 1st Lieutenant Chapman were right about one thing, they were being watched, but not by the Kiowa. It was the Apache. It was known to all white men who ever tangled with the Apache that when you didn't see them, they were watching you. Every trooper in the column searched the areas around them as they moved along keeping their eyes and ears open for any trouble, but of course they knew if trouble did come, especially from the Mescalero Apache, the only way you'd know that is when somebody died, or was wounded by them, but by the time you realize what was happening, it's too late, yet you do the best you can, any way you can to stay alive and above grass.

Then, an arrow flew. The arrow struck the driver of the last wagon in the chest causing him to be flung backwards into the wagon. Then, came the unmistaken war whoops from the Apache. They came right out of the ground, from behind trees. A few even sprang from dry gullies, ditches, crevasses, and arroyos. It was soon hand to hand fighting with Captain Locke shouting orders only to be unheard because of the fighting and gunfire. Lieutenant Chapman aimed and fired his service weapon at a Indian who was intent on clubbing Captain Locke who didn't notice the Indian coming up behind him. An Apache jumped on the last wagon in order to take off in it, but a trooper fired and the Indian fell over in the seat. The horses became spooked, so the wagon went careening off, out of line, and away from the column. Privates, Elvin Cates, and Tom Eppes noticed it, so they hurriedly went chasing after the wagon, but they had two Apache braves chasing after them. Corporal, Angus McQuarrie kicked his horse in the flanks and went riding hard after the two Apache braves who were riding hard after the two troopers, who were riding hard to catch the runaway wagon, in order to bring it back into the column. With his horse galloping as fast as he could, Corporal McQuarrie raised his service pistol and fired. He missed his intended target. He raised his weapon and fired again. The Apache, then pitched backwards, falling from his pony. The other brave turned his horse towards McQuarrie just in time to be hit with a bullet. The brave pitched sideways from the impact of the bullet, and fell from his pony. Privates Elvin Cates, and Tom Eppes gradually caught up to the runaway wagon and turned the horses back towards the column. Corporal McQuarrie caught up to them, and again they were confronted with Apache braves. As the Apache withdrew from the field of battle at the column, the men at the runaway wagon fired at the oncoming braves. There were four, now, there was one. He turned his pony, and began to flee. When Private Cates went to fire at him, Corporal McQuarrie hollered for him to let the brave go. Private Cates complained about that profusely, but Corporal Angus McQuarrie shut him up quick like.

Chapter Five

Don't seem quite fair

Captain Locke and 1st Lieutenant Chapman fired at the fleeing Apache. A couple braves fell from their ponies as they fled.

Captain Locke, then hollered, "Burglar, sound recall!"

The mounted troopers who had taken off after the fleeing Apache heard the bugle sound recall, so they reined their horses around, and rode back to the column. Lieutenant Chapman turned in his saddle to see that Corporal McQuarrie, Private Epps, and Private Cates was bringing the runaway wagon back to the column.

As Lieutenant Chapman turned back to Captain Locke, the captain yelled out, "Report, Lieutenant!"

Lieutenant Chapman replied, "I haven't the number of casualties yet, Captain."

Captain Locke, then said, "As soon as you have them, Lieutenant."

"Yes, Sir"

With that said, Lieutenant Chapman rode up and down the column collecting what was given as a casualty report. Lieutenant Chapman in just a few short minutes gathered that report. Then, Lieutenant Chapman rode back to where Captain Locke was waiting and gave him the casualty list. The list was three dead, and two wounded in an already dead and wounded patrol effort.

Captain Locke, then said, "This is not exactly how I thought this patrol would go, Lieutenant."

Lieutenant Chapman replied, "Does it ever, Captain?"

Captain Locke scoffed saying, "Point well taken, Lieutenant. Point taken. Well, Lieutenant, let's gather the dead and put them amongst the rest, then move out."

Lieutenant Chapman replied, "Yes, Sir." He reined his horse away from Captain Locke and hollered, "1st Sergeant! Gather them up, if you please, and prepare to move out."

Some distance away, 1st Sergeant, Gene Ralston replied, "Yes, Sir."

1st Sergeant, Ralston reined his horse to ride along the line of wagons, and began to call out troopers to gather the recent dead, and then add them to the already dead.

1st Sergeant Gene Ralston, then addressed 2nd Lieutenant, Flint Conyers stating the column was ready to move out. Then, Lieutenant Conyers reported to 1st Lieutenant Chapman that the column was ready to move out, who in turn reported to Captain Locke of their readiness to move out.

Captain Locke, then hollered, "Let's move out!"

And, again the column slowly moved towards Fort Richardson, but with less men alive than

when they got to the ambush site. That fact lay heavy on Captain Gary Locke's mind. When the column had gone a few miles, Captain Locke turned the column south towards Gainesville, Texas, however, the column would bypass Gainesville, veering more to the west. Then,

Captain Locke would lead the column due west toward Sain't Jo, veering more to the southwest avoiding Sain't Jo altogether. Then, he would lead the column southwest towards Jacksboro and Fort Richardson. While in the meantime, 1st Lieutenant Lundstrom would lead his detail away from Whitesboro, Texas, due west to Ringgold Barracks out of Ringgold, Texas where the remnant of the Comanche ambush, commanded by Captain Philo Dobbs and company was garrisoned, and headquartered. Then, somewhere in between Gainesville and Sain't Jo, due to the delay by Indian attacks on the column commanded by Captain Gary Locke, the column and detail commanded by 1st Lieutenant Miles Lundstrom would certainly, and most inevitably cross trails.

Slim swung himself onto his saddle, then said, "Listen, Victor, since the cattle has settled down, and no longer in any danger of being rustled, I should be home. I have a mother and a sister who needs me there, especially now. You think you know why."

Victor Corman replied, "I do. You go on home, Slim. We'll take care of things here."

Slim, then said, "Thanks, Victor." Pointing to the newly dug grave, Slim said, "I'm sorry for that."

Victor turned to the grave of Greg Hickman saying, "Yeah. We are too, Slim."

With that said, Slim reined his horse away from the homestead camp, and nosed his horse for home.

When Slim rode onto the homestead front court yard near the bunkhouse, Mike Eagan was leaning against an upright four by four support for the attached roof.

Slim, then said, "You alright?"

Mike answered, "Right as rain, Slim. Just a little sore, is all, but I'll get over it. I had to get out of that bunkhouse even if for a few minutes. Walls started closin' in on me."

Slim noticed Eric wasn't outside, or anywhere near Mike.

Slim asked, "Where's Eric, Mike. He should be close in case you fall, or somethin'."

Mike replied, "He's in the house. He was needed for something."

Slim said, "In the house, huh?"

Slim dismounted, then led his horse to the corral, and tossed the lines over the top rail. He turned and walked back to the bunkhouse.

As he walked up to Mike, Slim said, "You should be layin' down, Mike. I bet your head is just swimmin'."

"Nah." Mike said. "Head's fine. Side's gettin' better. I can't lay down just now. I feel all stove up. Need to stretch myself."

Slim, then said, "Well, don't do too much stretchin', or you'll open up that wound again."

Mike replied, "I don't think so. It's more hurt than anything else, Slim."

Slim turned and looked towards the house, asking, "I wonder what it was they needed Eric for?"

Mike replied, "I couldn't say, Slim. I wasn't told. He just said he was needed in the house."

"Hmm." Slim replied. "I expect I should go find out. But first you go to your bunk. No

need to lie down, just be on your bunk while I go find out. I don't want you movin' 'round without…"

Mike butted in saying, "Yeah, I know, Mother hen. So, go on with you. I'll be fine as frog's hair. 'Sides, I'll soon be as strong as an ox."

"Oxen sometimes die."

"Well, now, ain't you a wealth of comfort?" Mike waved Slim off saying, "Aw, get out a here."

"I'll be back soon enough, and you best be sittin' on your bunk, or you and I will have a heart-to-heart talk."

When Slim entered the house, the door latched behind him as he went into the living room.

Up against the window that looked out onto the main yard of the Homestead lay his father, Richard, in his casket dressed in his best bib 'n tucker surrounded by an array of assorted colors and types of flowers. Slim walked up to gaze upon his late father as he lay there with pennies over his eyes. Slim smiled as he reached out and touched the stone coldness of his father's hand. He quickly withdrew his touch. Slim looked down at his father with a look of lost at his father. Slim turned, then he noticed the living room was empty, but a second, or two later Jenny and their mother, Mae, came into the living room from her and Richard's bedroom.

Slim asked, "Well now, what have you two been up to?"

"Oh," Mae replied, as she put her hand to her chest, "just packin' up some of your dad's things, like his clothes, boots, belts, and other things that are no longer needed. I've kept what I want to remind me of him." She whimpered, then said, "The rest of his things you can pilfer through and keep what you want."

"I wouldn't call it pilferin', Mom. Selection, would be the word I would use."

"Call it what you will." Mae replied. "It amounts to the same thing."

Mae stopped in her tracks, looked at Slim who bore the hurt of her words and implications. She teared up and went to him in quick fashion.

Burying her head in his chest, she cried out, "I'm so sorry, Danny. Please forgive your blubberin' ol' fool of a woman and her hurtful words."

As Mae sobbed against his chest, Jenny stood idly by with tears in her eyes. Jenny looked at Slim as tears ran down her face and noticed that he too had tears in his eyes. He wrapped his arms around his mother, and whispered sweet comforting words into the top of her head. Just then, Eric came through the back door with an arm load of firewood. He, then stepped into the living room from the kitchen only to find the tender scene between Slim, Jenny, and Mae Siringo. Slim had noticed Eric, but said nothing. Eric, on the other hand, politely backed his way out of the living room.

Then, horses' hooves were heard coming onto the Homestead front court yard. Slim released his embrace, turned to look out of the front window onto the yard, and couldn't believe who it was. Devin Wade, and he brought friends. He drew his holstered weapon and checked the loads in his pistol. Satisfied, Slim closed the bullet latch to his revolver, then re-holstered it. Slim went to the front door, and opened it. As the door latched behind him, he stood erect on the front porch, waiting for what was to come.

Slim spoke in an aggressive manner, asking, "What do you want here, Wade?"

Wade replied, "To tell you the God's honest truth, I don't rightly know, Danny, or is it, Slim, now days?"

Slim answered, "Either one will do. So, again what is it you want?"

"Like I said, I don't rightly know, but it did occur to me that your late father, Richard, had passed away, and I came to pay my last respects, uh, with your permission of course."

"Permission denied, Wade." Slim, then said. "Now, were I you, I'd get off my land as soon as you come on it. Now, git."

Wade stared hard at Slim, then turned his head one way, then another surveying the area around him. One of his men reached for his holstered weapon, but Wade hollered at him.

"Don't be a fool, Keith. He'll drop you before you clear leather."

Keith became angry saying, "You have a lot of faith in me, don't you, Wade?"

Wade replied, "Not really, no. Not when it comes to Slim Siringo I don't. Plus, there's probably a few guns on us right now. Am I right, Slim?"

Slim answered, "I wouldn't be surprised, Wade. Now, git movin'."

Keith stared angrily at Slim, then said, "There will be another time, Slim."

Slim replied, "That's, Mister Slim to you."

That angered Keith even more, but Wade denied him his satisfaction, at least for the moment. Keith could wait another day to die.

Wade, then said, "We're leavin' now, but rest assured, *Danny*, you come to town, you'll leave in the same kind of box your dad is in. I hope I made myself clear."

Slim chided, "You did. Now, I'm tired a talkin'."

Wade gave a knee jerk reaction expecting Slim to draw and fire, but he didn't. Wade relaxed enough to smile, they then reined their horses out of the front court yard of the Siringo homestead. When the threat of Wade and his hired guns were gone, Mike came from the bunkhouse carrying a Henry repeating rifle. Slim looked behind him, to his left, to the side of the house, and there he saw Eric with his pistol in hand beside a tree he was using for cover. Eric came from the tree up to Slim, breathing a heavy sigh of relief.

Mike broke the stillness by saying, "That was close, don't you think?"

Slim replied with a nervous chuckle, "Yeah. Too close."

Eric, then said, "But we was ready for 'em, wasn't we?"

Slim replied, "In a manner of speakin', yes, you could say that."

Eric smiled at Slim saying, "As long as you agree, I'm good with that."

Slim turned to Mike, "How you doin'?"

Mike smiled, then answered, "Right as rain, Slim."

Slim, then said, "Good. Now, git back in there."

Brass Tacks was seated at a table in the Dancing Bear saloon with, Lilah Silko, his girl and informant. She was sitting on his lap, squealing with pleasure and joy of having Brass Tacks back again, only she called him by his given name… Lane Talbot.

Brass Tacks, then said, "Hey, Mateo, how 'bout have another bottle of Tequilla, eh, Senior?"

In his broken English, Mateo answered, "Comin' right up, Senior Lane."

Lane turned his attention to Lilah, saying, "And, you, my little chickadee. How 'bout you give Brass Tacks a little dance?"

Lilah became pouty and gloomy saying, "I hate the name, Brass Tacks. What does that name mean anyways?" She snuggled up closer to him, saying, "Why not use your given name? Lane Talbot. What's wrong with that name, huh?"

Ignoring Lilah's question, Lane tossed her from his lap, then said, "Dance, for me my little Chiquita. Dance for me. Lane Talbot."

Amidst the hoots and hollers, a great smile spread across her face as Mateo tossed her a couple of castanets.

She stood with her feet apart, but soon, she was twirling and spinning around the room with her skirt flapping in the breeze caused by her dancing, plus the castanets sounding. Clickety- Clack. Clickety-Clack.

Suddenly, someone threw a Mexican sombrero onto the floor not far from her, scaring up the dust. She smiled as she stared at it. She, then gave Lane an alluring look, then, with sheer delight spread across her face as she stepped onto the sombrero and began to dance the Mexican Hat dance. Then, Lane and a few of his men, plus those men already in the saloon, and the sound of those castanets. The men began to serenade her with their hoots and hollers begging her for more as she spun one way, then twirled another. Her feet were moving as fast as a snake striking, but she never stepped out of the crease of that sombrero. Soon, they wasn't just hooting and hollering, but they began to clap, and stomped their feet in their appreciation of the dance from this beautiful Mexican maiden. But in all actuality, she was a Yaqui maiden. Lilah, then leaped off of the sombrero, and twirled. Her body then just collapsed with her feet disappearing under her. When it looked like her butt hit the floor, she dropped her head to her chest, then quickly she raised it with a smile on her face. Her body heaved, breathing hard from doing such a stupendous hat dance. The castanets were silent. The crowd erupted with more hoots, and hollers while clapping their hands, and stomping their feet. She sprang to her feet and headed for the table where Lane was sitting, but a man from out of the crowd grabbed her by the left wrist. Lilah spun her head to stare at the man with wild eyes. The man wore a lusty grin.

The man said, "Lane Talbot ain't nobody, sweet cheeks. Do a little dance for me, honey. Harley Coates."

Feigning anger, Lane looked on as this man grabbed Lilah's wrist, and cringed at what the man said. Lane slowly came to his feet and faced the man named Harley Coates. Each man snarled at the other, bared their teeth at each other, and gave the other man threatening moves towards the other. Lilah finally broke free from the man's grasp, and stepped away in a hurry. Brass Tacks men jumped to their feet, pulled their weapons and pointed them at this man called, Harley Coates. Harley Coates stared at five weapons pointed at him, and again he snarled. Behind the bar, Mateo began pulling bottles of whiskey, and Tequilla from the shelf against the wall behind him, and was putting the bottles under the bar for safe keeping. The men in the saloon, other than Lane's men, began to run for cover. Lane, and the man, Harley Coates, squared off against each other. Then, surprisingly, the two men smiled, then, they roared with laughter. Confusion spread across the faces of Lane's men, as well as, the face of Lilah Silko. Lane and Harley Coates came together and shook hands vigorously.

Lane, then shouted, "Harley, you ol' horse thief. What brings you to Waco?"

Harley replied, "Just passin' through. Then, I saw you come in here. So, how 'bout you? What brings you here?"

Just then, Lilah came running over, and was complaining to Lane, "You goin' to let him get away with putting his hands on me, Lane?"

Harley replied, "Sorry, Dearie, but I had to get Lane's attention."

Lane said, "You did that, Harley."

Lilah, then said, "You could a got his attention by doin' somethin' else, you know?"

Harley replied, "Of course, but you were the best attention getter at the time."

Lilah scoffed, then said, "I don't like him, Lane. Tell him to go away."

Lane replied, "But Lilah, he's a good friend. I can't tell him what, and what not to do."

Lilah, again, scoffed, then said, "In that case."

Lilah turned abruptly, and hurriedly walked away, mumbling to herself as she left.

Lane asked, "Where you goin'?"

Lilah shouted back over her shoulder, "Where he ain't."

Lane and Harley smiled as they watched her until she had disappeared into the next room.

Harley, then said, "I regret to say this, but I have that effect on most women."

Lane chuckled heartily, then replied, "Ah, Harley. Always with the wit of the tongue."

Lane, who was smiling, casually turned to his men who held their weapons on Harley. Losing his smile, Lane said, "Did you not hear me when I said, Harley was a friend? We do not hold our weapons on friends, so put those things away."

The men who were standing around Brass Tacks slowly, but surely, holstered their weapons, then sat back down in their seats. The men with Brass Tacks were wary of this man, Harley Coates, whom they just now found out was a friend of Lane Talbot. One could only guess at what each man was thinking. Most likely they were wondering why Lane had not mentioned this man before now? Who is Harley Coates anyway? Could he be a childhood friend Lane grew up with, or could it be he was a part of the business adventures of gun running that Lane started sometime back? Could he be an ex-partner who took off on his own? Time will tell if he is a friend in deed, or a friend in need. He has yet to say what his business with Lane is.

Harley, then said, "You never did say why you're here in Waco, Lane. You on the hunt for somethin'?"

Lane replied, "Yeah, but the somethin' is too sensitive, and there are too many ears in here to discuss it here and now."

"Ah, well, no matter." Harley said. "The thing is you're here, and that's all that matters, right? We can talk of old times, you and I away from that missy you got yourself tangled with."

Lane replied, "Lilah? She's one of the reasons I'm here. She can tell me things that I need to know 'bout 'round here, and it could bring more money my way."

"Really?" Harley asked. "Then, she's the one to know when money could be had."

Lane, then said, "She's my eyes and ears here in Waco. She hears everything that comes and goes in and 'round here, Harley, and when I come in, she gives me the information. I, then, decide one way, or the other which one is a good thing to go after."

Harley looked at the bottle of whiskey, then Lane said, "Help yourself. There's more where that came from."

Harley replied, "Thanks."

Harley picked up the bottle of whiskey and poured himself two fingers of the rot gut, then he down it in one gulp. He gritted his teeth at the strong liquid, as the fire lit up his tongue. As Harley put his whiskey glass down on the table, a man dressed in leather, and had the aroma of dried blood and guts came into the saloon.

As he walked up to the bar, Mateo backed away from the bar saying, "Good Lord, Senior. Did ever think of gettin' yourself a bath before comin' in here? You stink to high heavens."

"I figured on getting' my first drink before I have that bath. Whiskey, senior, and I'll have the bottle."

Mateo went to say somethin', but Harley spoke saying, "How 'bout you go take a bath first, Mister. You're ruining the taste of good whiskey. You smell somethin' awful."

The man turned to Harley, then said, "Me and my partner just came out of the Wichita Mountains huntin' buff'ler, and takin' skins where we can. Been at it for near six months, and I expect to have my drink. Then, I'll be takin' a bath, and then, I'll have a bite to eat. Tired of my own cookin'. I won't be long, Mister."

Harley, then said, "It's already been too long. I suggest you move on before you git hurt."

The buffalo hunter, then said, "Don't push me, Mister. I done said I won't be long."

This buffalo hunter stood five foot nothing, but wide at the shoulders like a four foot wide tree trunk. The size of this man didn't addle Harley though. He tangled with far worse looking men than this man once, or twice, and he came out on the lucky end of the fight. He figured he could do the same with this old buffalo hunter, and mountain man of sorts with no problem whatsoever. So, he pushed, and harassed the man until the buffalo hunter had had enough of Harley. He was agitated to the point that he challenged Harley to back up his words.

As Harley stood to his feet, he told Lane, "This won't take long."

Lane, then said, "No buttin' in, boys. This is Harley's doin'. Not ours."

The two men squared off against each other, and they sized each other up. Then, they slowly began to circle. Those men who were in the saloon backed their way from the fight that was deemed to happen. Lane and his men remained seated as to enjoy the entertainment. If one, or the other man died, that was too bad, but it was just icing on the cake for what was about to happen according to Lane. Death was no stranger to these men, and the spilling of blood did not scare them, except for their own. The buffalo hunter looked up into the eyes of Harley, who stood six foot three, towering over the man. Without laying a hand on each other, Harley took a step back, then drew his pistol, and cocked it.

The buffalo hunter then pulled his knife from the scabbard in his belt, and that made Harley scoff, and chuckle a little.

Harley, then said, "Who brings a knife to a gun fight, little man? Besides, you think I

want your filth all over me?"

The buffalo hunter replied, "If I'd a known this was goin' to happen, I would a brought my rifle."

Harley pointed at the man, then said, "So, all you have is that there knife?"

The buffalo hunter replied, "Don't seem quite fair, does it?"

Harley smiled, then said, "Ah, hell, who says life's fair anyways?"

Just then, a man came bounding through the saloon doors. As he came through doors, the man saw the two men in a quarrel.

Confused, the man, then asked, "Say, what goes on here, Rufus?"

Harley twirled around, pointing his weapon at the man. The man stopped abruptly, throwing both hands in the air. Just then, the man named Rufus shove his knife into Harley's ribs. Harley flinched sideways from the knife being stuck in his ribs. Then, the other man rushed over and took the gun from Harley's hand.

Harley turned back towards the man named Rufus, only to have Rufus stick him again, low in the belly. Harley's eyes bugged out, and his mouth flew open, but no sound came out. Rufus smiled as Harley tumbled to the saloon floor. The man stood still, and unmoving as he stared in unbelief at Rufus, then looked at the man lying on the floor in his own pool of blood.

Mateo looked out over the bar saying, "Ay, Chihuahua, look at that mess. Ay, caramba!"

The man, then asked, "What have you done, Rufus? What have you done?"

Rufus replied, "It was self-defense, Jud. You saw he had a gun in his hand. By the way, thank you."

"Me? What did I do?" Jud asked.

"If it weren't for you coming in when you did, he would a shot me, and that gave me the chance to do what I did, defend myself."

"You took advantage of my entrance just to kill a man, Rufus."

"I told you I was defending myself, Jud." Rufus proclaimed. "I defended myself."

The men of Brass Tacks stood to their feet seconds before Lane did. Lane shook his head easy like as he walked over to stand a few feet from Rufus and Jud. However, before Lane could speak, Deputy Sheriff, Howard Dunsberry, followed closely by Sheriff, A.K. Masters came bounding through the saloon doors.

Both men had their weapons cocked, and at the ready.

Sheriff, A.K. Masters growled, "All right, what goes on in here?"

Then, both men looked down at Harley lying on the floor in a pool of blood with Rufus standing over him holding a knife, and Jud was holding a gun.

Deputy Sheriff, Dunsberry, then yelped, "Lord have mercy."

Sheriff, Masters grabbed the gun from Jud's hand saying, "Who did what here?"

Lane spoke saying, "I could tell you if you want me to, Sheriff."

Sheriff Masters, then asked, "I take it you saw what happened?"

Lane chuckled, then said, "Sheriff, everybody saw what happened. Me, and my boys here saw everything what was to see, as well as these in the saloon."

Sheriff Masters replied, "Then, how 'bout you tell me what happened, Mister. This fella has a knife, and I just took this gun from this man's hand."

Lane, then said, "I must admit the dead man was a friend a mine, but I also must admit he wrangled this buffalo hunter into a fight. What he had in mind was to kill the buffalo hunter. It of course would've been murder. The man defended hisself against, Harley Coates."

Sheriff Masters said, "This man is Harley Coates?"

Lane replied, "Yep, that's him alright. Harley Coates."

Deputy Sheriff, Dunsberry, then asked, "Just who are you, Mister, and how is it Harley Coates is a friend a yours?"

Lane answered, "The name's, Prescott. Wiley Prescott. Me and Harley grew up together. I hadn't seen him in years till just a few minutes ago. We shared a drink together, and then, this buffalo hunter come waltzin' in here stinkin' up the place. Harley there took offence to it. Well, you're lookin at the result of that offence. I heard he wound up on the wrong side of the law." He scoffed, then added, "It's too bad he had to end up this way by a buffalo hunter."

Sheriff Masters turned to Mateo Sanchez, bartender, asking, "Is that how you saw it, Mateo?"

Mateo swallowed hard, then said, "Si, Senior Sheriff. Just as he says. Ay, caramba! What a mess, I think!"

Sheriff Masters, then said, "A couple of you men help take this man's body over to the undertaker."

Then, the saloon doors slapped back and forth when Herschel Davis, the owner of the Dancing Bear saloon, entered the saloon. Herschel looked shocked at what he was seeing.

As Harley was being carried from the saloon, Herschel asked, "What in God's name is goin' on here, Sheriff? What's the meanin' of all this? And, who are these two men?"

Before Sheriff Masters could answer, Lane growled, "Howdy, Herschel."

Herschel smiled, then said, "Why you ol' coyote, where you been?"

As the two men shook hands vigorously, Sheriff Masters asked, "So, you two know each other? Uh, don't tell me, you and Herschel here, and that man Harley Coates grew up together?"

Herschel looked back towards the saloon doors, then said, "That was Harley?"

Masters looked at Herschel out of his peripheral looking for a reaction.

Sheriff Masters, then replied, "It's who Wiley Prescott here says he is."

Herschel looked confused, but asked, "You say, Wiley Prescott?"

Lane spoke, saying, "Yeah, me. You know I had to speak up 'bout what happened, and who did what didn't I?"

Herschel replied, feigning surprise, "Of course you did, Wiley. It just surprised me to know the sheriff knew your name."

"He asked," shrugging his shoulders, "so, I told him. I saw nothin' wrong with that."

Herschel, then said, "And, why would you? You're an honest man, Wiley, and a man who

always stands for the law."

Lane patted Herschel on the left arm friendly like, saying, "Thanks, my friend. I do try to."

Sheriff Masters, then said, "Uh, huh." He turned to Jud and Rufus, saying, "Well, I think the two of you need to get out a here and for everybody's sake, go take a bath before you do anything else. At least jump in the creek so's you won't cause any more trouble. At least that'd be somethin'."

Jud replied, "We'll do 'er, Sheriff. And, right away, too." He grabbed Rufus by the arm, and began to pull him towards the door, saying, "C'mon Rufe. You heard what the Sheriff said. Let's get out a here."

Rufus refused, saying, "I ain't had my drink yet, Jud." He shook himself free from Jud's grip on his arm. "I ain't leavin' till I do, Jud."

Deputy Dunsberry said, "It's either you leave now, or you'll spend the night in jail."

Rufus replied, "Hmm." Then, he looked at deputy Dunsberry through his peripherals.

Rufus asked, "How good's breakfast?"

Both Sheriff Masters and Deputy Dunsberry looked stunned, then they chuckled.

Sheriff Masters, then said, "Now, I've heard everything. Someone who may go to jail for

the night asks how good is breakfast. That's funny."

Deputy Dunsberry replied, "It's the first for me too, Sheriff."

Mateo took the bottle of whiskey and sat it down on the bar, saying, "Here, Senior. Please, please, take the bottle and leave. Have your drink somewhere else. Ay, caramba!"

Rufus took the bottle of whiskey that Mateo allowed him to have, then asked, "Is there a glass that goes with it?"

Mateo replied, "Jes, there's a glass." Pointing to the glasses on the bar, he said, "Ready and waiting, Senior. Please, take one and leave. The smell is too fierce." He waved his hand vertically in front of his face, saying, "Ay, Chihuahua!"

Sheriff Masters, then said, "Well, Howard, it seems we're done here, unless Mister Prescott here has anything else to say?."

"There's nothin' else to say, Sheriff. Sorry, I have nothin'."

Herschel said, "Mateo, for Pete's sake, open up all these windows and such, and air this place out. It stinks like somethin' awful in here."

Speaking to Rufus and Jud, Sheriff Masters, then said, "All right you two, let's go."

Sheriff Masters went to put his hand on the back of Rufus to hurry them along, then quickly decided against it. He looked at his hand in revulsion, then dropped it down by his side.

Deputy Sheriff, Howard Dunsberry looked at Sheriff Masters, shaking his head while rolling his eyes in disgust. When Sheriff Masters and Deputy Dunsberry left the saloon behind Jud Briscoe and Rufus Costello, Lilah Silko came back into the room. Lane and his merry men reseated themselves.

As she sat on Lane's lap, Lane asked, "Did you enjoy the floor show, my dear, or were you too afraid to watch?"

Lilah acted excited, then said, "I am glad that man is dead. I did not like him. Not one bit."

Lane chuckled, then replied, "It ain't nice to speak ill of the dead, Lilah. Not good."

Lilah kicked her feet in the air, then said, "You think I give one," Snapping her finger, "for that man? Huh? I tell you, no."

Lane squeezed her, then asked lustfully, "Why is it you stir me so?"

Lilah squealed with delight, then replied, "Because I am beautiful, and…"

Lane squeezed her again as he butted in saying, "You certainly are that."

Again, Lilah squealed with delight, then continued, "And, I have information for you. Important information, I think."

Lane said, "Well, let's have it, Lilah, and I will certainly make it worth your while."

Lilah looked at Lane asking, "How much is that worth, worth?"

Lane replied, "Very generous, but wouldn't that depend on the information you have in order to know how much that worth is worth?"

Lilah stared at Lane with suspect, then said, "You have double talk."

Lane replied, "Double talk? If memory serves me well, it was you who started the double talk. How much is that worth, worth? I just answered your double talk."

Lilah yelled out, "Then, how much is that worth, worth?"

Lane answered in like fashion, "I don't know! Will you stop all this double talk, and tell me what kind of information you have for me?"

Slim Siringo 'A Brimful of Nettle'

Chapter Six

Chaotic Noise

It wasn't long until Devlin Wade stepped away from his office at the rear of the Red Dust saloon in Comanche, Oklahoma, and ventured out into the main room. At this time of day, the saloon was near full of patrons. The piano player was pounding out a ragtime song. A song called, 'Frog Legs Rag'. A lively tune. He took a cheroot from his jacket pocket, then took a match and lit his cigar. When he got to the bar, he turned to see Paul Stroud sitting at a table with a bottle of whiskey adorning the table. He turned further to his left and saw Karl Stokes also sitting at a table. Both were most likely intoxicated. He, then noticed Cecil Haywood, and Larry Kimber enter the saloon, and all of a quick, he had an idea.

Wade turned to Fred Eubanks, bartender, "Let's have a bottle Fred. My finest."

"Yes, Sir."

Fred turned towards the wall behind him, and grabbed a bottle off the wall shelf. He turned and put the bottle on the bar.

Fred said, "There you are, Wade. Your finest."

Wade grabbed the bottle from the bar, then said, "Thanks, Fred."

"Yes, Sir. Anytime."

Fred, then wandered down the length of the bar to help a customer with his drink order.

Wade turned from the bar, pointed at Cecil Haywood, and then at Larry Kimber. He waved for them to follow him to his office. Larry and Cecil did follow Wade, but Wade stopped short of his office to a dark secluded corner.

Wade, then asked, "You fellas know where the Silver Shovel Silver Mine is?"

Cecil replied, "I do."

Larry also replied, "I do as well, Wade. I believe it's Amos Stegner, and Seth Brubaker's silver mine, is it not?"

Wade snapped, "It's not their mine. It's my mine. They're in serious trouble from me."
Cecil asked, "Your mine, Wade?"

Wade answered, "Yes, my mine. They're taking silver from my mine, and they're livin'

high on the hog with my silver, not to mention the gold, and that needs to stop as of right now."

Larry asked, "So, how do we do that?"

Wade smiled, then said, "A night raid on the mine to get rid of Amos Stegner and Seth Brubaker, but not before they sign over their mine to me."

Larry, then asked, "How do we do that?"

Wade said, "I don't care how you do it, just get their signatures on this deed of transfer."

Cecil, then asked, "So, what then?"

Wade replied, "Then, all mines have cave-ins, right?"
Cecil, then said, "Ah, I got ya, Boss. A cave-in will cover a lot of evidence."

Larry said, "Yeah. Dead men tell no tales."

Wade said, "The sun will be down in about an hour, so take a few men, and give those yahoos at the silver mine a visit. And, don't come back without them having their signatures on that deed of transfer to me, and then, them disappearing in a mine cave-in."

Cecil replied, "We'll get 'er done, Wade."

Sitting around the already made campfire, a coffee pot was hanging from a skewering rod. Amos Stegner and Seth Brubaker were preparing their supper, and getting ready for a night's rest. After a harrowing day of sweat, sore and aching muscles stemming from strenuous labor, these men were ready to end their day. The Silver Shovel Silver mine was located in a coulee, which is a dry stream bed, or, a ravine that once carried melt water from a glacier. The entrance to the mine was located nearly halfway up from bottom of that coulee. The diggings had several sections of wooden planks in support of a wooden slough in case any gold flakes, or nuggets that came forth from mining the silver, and a few assorted picks and shovels, and a couple of wheel barrows. As the two men sat on a rock, or, a tree limb with their plates full of beans and side meat (sow belly), and a cup of coffee. The bread to slop up the juice of the beans was, 'Shanty-boat bread', or, 'Lazy Man's bread', however you want to call it. No matter what you call it, there was no yeast in the bread, and the bread was baked in a cast iron skillet sitting on a trivet, surrounded, as well as, covered with heated coals. It had gotten dark rather quickly. The two men had finished their supper and had settled down for a goodnights rest. Each man had erected his own lean-to as to not disturb the other by the man's own restlessness during the night. Silver ore deposits, as well as any gold they found were kept in saddlebags at the back of each man's lean-to.

Then, out of the darkness came the sound of many hooves. The pounding of horses' hooves was so loud it had awakened the two men who were asleep. They sat up in their bedrolls, and were trying to adjust to the dark. The sound of hoof beats came closer, and closer.

Seth asked, "What in tarnation is goin' on?"

Amos replied, "Sounds like we're 'bout to have company."

Seth, then said, "At this hour?"

Amos replied, "The onliest low down critter what does that is claim jumpers. How 'bout we give 'em a warm welcome? Hot lead."

Then, the two men swept their blankets aside, and dashed to retrieve their rifles. Once they had laid their hands on their weapons, they made sure those weapons were loaded and ready for use. As the sound of horses' hooves came closer, both men separated. Seth hid behind a large fallen tree limb, while Amos dropped on his belly at the top the coulee for cover. They were mere yards apart when the sound of horses' hooves suddenly stopped. Each man trained their eyes to adjust to the darkness. It became eerily quiet. Every so often they could hear rustling in the bushes close by, but no footfalls were heard. It was a cool evening, but with the situation these men were facing, sweat broke out on each man's forehead and face. The sweat began to sting their eyes and blur their vision, and the salt in the sweat caused their eyelids to close taking away their sight. They took a rag and wiped away the sweat from their face. The palms of their hands started to sweat. The wait for something to happen was becoming nerve racking. The not knowing what was going to happen was also a factor in their nervousness. From the sound of the horse' hooves there must've been at least twenty, thirty horses coming their way. Where are they? Did they go on by? The answer to those questions would all too soon be answered in a way that would terrify both men. But for the moment they were safe behind cover, and they were ready for trouble. Weapons locked and loaded for bear. The moon had set high in the sky giving off lengthening shadows. The itch to move and find out where those riders went had taken hold of Amos. He looked one way, then the other, He nervously figured he had the advantage because he knew how to get around their diggings even in the dark. He moved without noise to where Seth had taken cover. Hunkered down in the dark, Amos crept his way towards Seth. Seth heard the almost silent footfalls of sand under foot. He cocked his weapon not knowing who was coming at him in the dark. Seth pointed his weapon in Amos' direction just as Amos appeared out of the darkness. Seth turned his weapon away from Amos, un-cocked it, and gave a heavy sigh of relief.

Seth whispered, "I almost shot you, you dad blamed fool. What 'er you doin' sneakin' 'round anyways? I could a killed ya."

Amos whispered, "Aw, I ain't sneakin'. I figured if they was claim jumpers, they'd a done tried it already. I don't know if they went on by, or not, so I figured I would find out."

"You tryin' to get yourself shot? You go out there with that moon castin' shadows, you just might as well say shoot me. I almost shot ya myself."

Amos, and Seth looked out into the darkness in all directions, seeing, or hearing nothing.

Amos whispered saying, "I don't like just sittin' here waitin' for the inevitable."

Seth replied, "It's better than dyin'. Get back over where you was."

"I'll go, but I won't like it."

"Just as long as you go is all that matters."

Amos looked out into the darkness, then as quiet as he could, he crept back to his position at the topside of the coulee.

When Amos left him, Seth whispered, "Cantankerous ol' fuss budget."

As soon as Amos got to his position at the coulee, he had a knee jerk reaction to what sounded like a spur striking a rock not far from him.

He became instantly aware that death was stalking him. Then, no sound whatsoever. He strained his ears to hear something, anything, but he heard nothing. No sound of a rustling bush. No footfalls separating sand under foot. No sticks, nor twigs snapping, and breaking. He kept his eyes staring into the darkness wanting to see any kind of movement. Nervous anxiety crept into Amos. It showed plainly on his face. His skin crawled under his clothes. He became fidgety, wanting to move. He flexed his fingers on the rifle he was holding. His hands became cold, and clammy. Sweat ran down into his eyes blinding him again. He hurriedly wiped his eyes with the rag. He developed a nervous twitch. It was so quiet a cricket would break the silence. Then, Amos heard a twig snap close to him to his right. He spun to fire, but the man fired first as he came out of the darkness. There was a loud groan as Amos fell onto the bank of the coulee. He slowly slid down to the bottom of the coulee all sprawled out on his back, blood staining his shirt front. He had his eyes opened, but looked out into nothing. Then, the man who shot him slipped back into the brush under the cover of darkness. Across the way from where Amos had positioned himself in the coulee, Seth wondered who took that shot. It didn't sound like Amos' rifle. His rifle had a clear and distinctive sound to it. He wanted to yell out for Amos, but he didn't want to give his position away. Seth had been exhibiting the same peculiar effects Amos had been exhibiting. Sweaty, clammy hands. Nervous anxiety. His skin seemed to be crawling under his clothes. Sweat ran down into his eyes causing him to hurriedly wipe away the sweat with his rag. Still no sound. Seth crawled to a cleft in the rock where he positioned himself aptly to defend himself if need be, but he hoped in the darkness, his position would not be compromised. He would wait till daybreak, then go hunting for those who did this dastardly deed, one, or two men at a time. The only person who would even venture a raid such as this was Devlin Wade. He wasn't sure if Amos was alive, or not, but he dared not find out. He knew he had to survive in order to serve recompense upon those who did this deed if took him the rest of his life to do it.

The next morning, somewhere around six o'clock, the coffee pot was boiling on the wood stove, while biscuits were baking in the oven. Mae was crumbling pork sausage into a cast iron skillet to brown in preparation to make biscuits and sausage gravy for breakfast. After raiding the hen house, she also fashioned to fry eggs to however they each wanted their eggs fried. Just a little after six, Jenny came into the kitchen.

Jenny said, "Oh, Mom, you don't need to do this. I can do this. You need to rest."

Mae turned to Jenny asking, "What in tarnation for? 'Sides, I ain't tired. I slept all night, well, most of it anyways."

Jenny replied, "I know. I heard you in… talking to dad. I cried."

Mae replied, "So did I. This takes my mind off of it, at least for a while. I can't always walk around grievin'. Ain't proper. I expect there will be more tears at Richard's funeral. Has Danny said when that would be?"

"I haven't heard a word, Mom. I don't think Danny is ready to put Pop under grass just yet. He has so much on his mind these days, what with Devlin Wade givin' us such a hard time of it. Why, Wade even came out here last night to pay his last respects to dad, but Danny told him to git, and never come back on Homestead land again."

Mae replied, "So, that's who that was? Good for Danny. Glad I didn't know that. I'd a given him a piece of my mind, let me tell you." She chuckled, then added, "Possibly even an ounce of lead, or two." She laughed heartily.

Jenny chuckled, "Oh, Mother! You are just so sly, and devilish at times. Sometimes I wonder where you got it."

Mae answered, "My mother. Your grandmother. She was somethin'. Strong as a whippin' stick, and yet, she could bend like a willow in the wind if need be. Proud woman. Proud she was. Never went lookin' for trouble, but she never backed down from trouble either. Too many brothers to stand up to with pure backbone I reckon."

Jenny replied, "I must admit she did have a strong constitution about her. She was soft spoken, caring, and lovable, but a whirlwind when she got angry."

"I miss her you know?" Mae, then said. "But my comfort lies in the fact that I'll be seeing her again. Could be soon."

Jenny turned abruptly to her mother saying, "Mother! Don't be sayin' things like that. We lost Randy, now dad. We don't need to lose you too."

Mae turned to her daughter saying, "Who says I'd be lost? The good Lord will put me just where he wants me, and that will be fine with my soul."

"That isn't exactly what I meant, Mom, and I think you know what I meant by saying that."

"Yes, Dear. I knew exactly what you meant."

"Well, don't be sayin' such things because I don't want to hear them."

"Just bein' logical, Honey. Everybody dies. It's just as natural as givin' birth, and even breathin'."

"Mom!?"

"Well, the old sayin' is, no one leaves this old world alive. A lot of folks before me have proven that point of view. Randy, now Richard has proven that."

"I wish you wouldn't say such things, Mom. I know they're true, but for me, please, don't talk 'bout such things."

"Okay, Honey. I won't if it bothers you that much."

"Thanks, Mom. It does bother me. Quite a bit. I hope you don't mind?"

Mae scoffed, then said, "Why should I mind? Me, talkin' 'bout my own demise? Shoot."

Satisfied, Jenny said, "Here, let me check the biscuits."

Mae replied, "They should be just 'bout done, They've been in the oven for 'bout ten minutes, or so."

Jenny opened the oven door, and as the heat of the oven caressed her face, she smiled saying, "Nice and golden brown, Mom. They'll be a tasty delight all smothered in butter, or hive honey."

"Well, you know me, Jenny. I like mine smothered in apple butter, and melted butter. That's good for what ails you, for certain."

Jenny grabbed a towel, and removed the biscuits from the oven, placing the pan on the table as Mae closed the oven door.

Then, without thinking, Jenny asked, "How was it Dad liked his bi…"

Jenny suddenly turned to her mother with a startled look on her face. Mae looked back with an understanding, and loving gaze. Jenny brought her hands to her mouth, then, almost in tears, she hurriedly left the kitchen.

Mae said, "Lord, please give us strength."

Just as Jenny left the room, Slim passed her, looking back at her.

He, then asked, "What's up with, Jenny, Mom?"

"Your dad, Danny. We were talkin' 'bout how Richard liked his biscuits, and it became too much for her."

Mae went on with her work, then, a few seconds later, Slim had poured himself a cup of coffee, then sat down at the table.

Mae looked back over her shoulder asking, "Have you come to a decision when your dad's buryin' will be? Hopefully soon. It's getting hard to see him lying there unable to move. It's heart breaking. It stirs your emotions. You have everything ready, don't you?"

Slim replied, "Yes, I do, Mom."

Mae turned to look at her son saying, "Then, let's get it done, Danny."

Slim lowered his head, then said softly, "We'll do 'er tomorrow."

Mae continued her work with no further words for her son, Danny. Slim waited until Mae made a couple of plates for Eric, and Mike who were in the bunkhouse.

She put those plates on a couple large trays as well as a cup of coffee each.

Slim put his coffee cup down on the table, then picked up these trays saying, "Thanks, Mom."

Then, Slim left the house with those plates on a tray to the bunkhouse. When he got to the bunkhouse, he found Eric out under the attached roof having a smoke. Eric smiled and tossed his rolled tobacco cigarette when he saw Slim with breakfast.

He rushed over to Slim saying, "Here, let me help you." When he grabbed one of the trays, he sniffed the air, then said, "Smells mighty good, Slim."

Slim replied, "Uh, huh. You're just lucky I made it here. I had almost made up my mind to have both plates for breakfast."

Eric said, "Aw, now, you wouldn't do that, would you? Leavin' me and Mike to go hungry?"

Slim answered, "Naw, I reckon not. How's he doin?"

Eric and Slim entered the bunkhouse, as Eric replied, "See for yourself."

Mike was sitting at the writing table just chomping at the bit for breakfast. When Slim and Eric entered the bunkhouse, Mike saw the plates of food, and smacked his lips in anticipation.

Mike said, "There's mine. Where's Eric's?"

Eric, then said, "Oh, ha, ha, ha. Ain't you funny."

Slim sat the tray of food on the table in front of Mike. Eric sat down at the table with his tray.

As both men began to eat their breakfast, Slim said, "I'd like to thank both a you for last night."

Between mouthfuls of food, Mike asked, "Last night?" He pulled one of the biscuits apart, then asked, "What happened last night?"

"When Wade came callin'."

Eric replied, "Oh, that." He gave slight of hand, then said, "Wasn't nothin'."

"Ain't the way I saw it, Eric. You and Mike here had my back. I thank you for that."

Mike then said, "No thanks necessary, Slim. We have more than enough to be thankful for here on the Homestead. You and your father have been more than generous to us. Especially to me."

Slim gave a wink to Eric, then said, "Aw, we'd do the same for any wounded animal, Mike."

Mike stopped chewing, looked at Eric, then said, "Ain't that the way it always is? Save a man's life and this is what he does."
Slim recoiled, then said, "You saved my life?"

Mike replied, "Sure. You yourself just said…"
Slim said, "I know what I said, Mike, and it wasn't thankin' you for savin' my bacon."

Mike, then said, "It might as well could've been. It amounts to the same thing, ya know."

Slim feigned anger, saying, "I'll leave you two to your breakfast and I'll leave before I get mad."

Mike, then said, "You can get mad and glad in the same pair a britches, ya know?"

As Slim left the bunkhouse, again, he gave a wink to Eric. Mike chuckled loudly.

When Slim left the bunkhouse, Mike, then said, "He's one of a kind, Eric. Ain't another man like him anywhere. Staunch. Proud. I ain't afraid to say he's my friend, or I his?" He points to his food with his fork saying, "Plus, his ma is right good cook."

Just before taking another bite of food, Eric said, "I'll be glad to let Riley know you said that."

1st Lieutenant, Miles Lundstrom was riding his horse ahead of the wagon of the wounded men of 2nd Lieutenant, Jamie Carlson's detail from Whitesboro, Texas. They were several miles from town on their way back to Ringgold Barracks near Ringgold, Texas. Lieutenant Lundstrom had bought three horses, and saddles from the town's hostler in Whitesboro with a voucher given to him by the quartermaster, per Colonel Mackenzie's orders for such an occasion. One for 2nd Lieutenant, Jamie Carlson, Army Scout, Ned Grayson, and Sergeant Major, Del Dickerson. Corporal, Jax MacDougall, Private, Clint Fairfield, and Private, Ernie Post were unable to sit a horse due to their wounds. They rode in the wagon.

Physician's Assistant, 2nd Lieutenant, Adam Murtaugh, along with Private, Spencer Ellsworth holding the reins to the draft horses, were sitting on the box seat of the wagon. Sergeant, Everett Sutrell rode alongside of the wagon while Sergeant Major Dickerson rode on the other side. Lieutenant Lundstrom turned to see Jamie who had his head bowed low, wiping his forehead with his neckerchief.

Lieutenant Lundstrom asked, "You all right, Lieutenant?"

Jamie replied, "A little light headed, Lieutenant. Eyes hurt. I'll be all right."

2nd Lieutenant Murtaugh yelled out, "He could use a rest, Lieutenant."

Lieutenant Lundstrom, then said, "I agree, Lieutenant Murtaugh. I think it best you ride in the wagon for a while to get your strength back. Rest your head, and drink plenty of water. You easterners ain't used to this Texas heat. It can do real hurt to you."

Then, Lieutenant Lundstrom called a halt, and the detail stopped.

Lieutenant Lundstrom said, "Let's take ten, Lieutenant. As I said, I think it best you ride in the wagon."

Jamie replied, "I'm all right, Lieutenant." Lieutenant Lundstrom then, said, "That wasn't a suggestion, Lieutenant. Lieutenant Murtaugh, make him as comfortable as possible, Sir."

"I'll do what I can, Lieutenant. It may not be much, but I will try."

"All that I ask, Lieutenant, is that you try."

Ten minutes later Jamie was sitting in the wagon at the rear gate, and each man was given a dipper of water from the water barrel to quench their thirst. 2nd Lieutenant, Murtaugh was examining each man's bandages, and he changed bandages where they were needed.

Lieutenant Lundstrom, then said, "Mister Grayson? Since you are an Army scout, please see what there is ahead of us trouble wise. I can't shrug off the feeling we're being followed."

"How far, Lieutenant?"

Lieutenant Lundstrom replied, "Oh, I'd say half a mile 'round-about would be sufficient, Mister Grayson."

"Half a mile 'round-about. Yes, Sir."

Ned reined his horse to the rear of the detail at least a half mile to see who it is, if anyone, could be following the detail. White man, or Indian.

Lieutenant Lundstrom, then hollered, "Sergeant Major?"

"Sir?" Sergeant Major Dickerson hollered back.

"The same as going ahead, Sergeant. Half a mile 'round-about. Get it done, Sergeant."

Sergeant Dickerson replied, "Yes, Sir."

Sergeant Dickerson kicked his horse in the flanks, and took off at a gallop going out in front of the detail in half a mile 'round-about tactic. Lieutenant Lundstrom rode to the rear gate of the wagon next to the horse Jamie was riding but was tethered at the rear of the wagon.

Sitting his horse, he asked, "Well, Lieutenant? Feelin' better?" He smiled.

As he soaked his bandage with water, Jamie replied, "Much better, Lieutenant. Thanks."

Lieutenant Lundstrom, then asked, "Think you can sit a horse, Lieutenant, with no problem, and not fall off?"

"I believe so, Lieutenant. I'd feel much better if I were on a horse, rather than in the back of this wagon."

"Well, then I give you leave to do so." Pointing to the tethered horse, he said, "Your mount is waiting."

Jamie replied, "Thank you, Sir."

Jamie dropped the rear gate, and exited the wagon. He, then stepped into the stirrup and swung himself onto the saddle.

He breathed deep, then smiled saying, "Ah, I feel much better, Lieutenant."

Lieutenant Lundstrom replied, "Good. Let's move out, Lieutenant Murtaugh."

Without a word spoken, Private Spencer Ellsworth slapped the reins over the backs of the draft horses, The wagon lurched backwards due to the forward pull of the draft horses. For the next hour, or hour and a half, they rode in silence, and happily, having no sign of trouble. Then, of a sudden, from the left of the detail came Ned Grayson, riding at full gallop. 1st Lieutenant Miles Lundstrom called a halt to the detail. The lieutenant sat on a dancing horse waiting for Ned Grayson to come up to him. Within a few seconds, Ned reined in, in front of the lieutenant, who sat eagerly awaiting the news Ned had concerning the safety of the men on this detail.

As Ned reined in, he said, "You was right, Lieutenant. We are bein' followed."

"By who, Grayson?" as he looked down his back trail.

"She'-te-quah. Sub-chief of the Chiricahua. He has 20 to 30 braves with him. He's just following at a distance. He stays to our rear keeping us at his front."

"What does that mean exactly? Following at a distance?"

"Only one thing, Lieutenant. They're more Indians ahead of us. How many, I don't know."

The lieutenant turned to see Sergeant Major Del Dickerson riding hard towards the detail.

The lieutenant turned back to Ned Grayson, then said, "Maybe he can tell us."

Ned turns to see Sergeant Dickerson riding hard their way, and coming on fast.

Ned said, "He seems to be in a hurry."

Lieutenant Lundstrom replied, "Weren't you?"

"Yeah, I suppose I was, but there was a reason."

Lieutenant Lundstrom, then said, "Well, let's hear what his reason is, shall we?"

Lieutenant Lundstrom and Ned Grayson, scout, waited for Sergeant Major Del Dickerson to arrive with news, which seemed to be very important, and urgent from the distance he's covering in such a short time. They waited, but not for long.

Sergeant Major Del Dickerson reined in in front of Ned and the lieutenant. He didn't salute the lieutenant. You never salute an officer in the field. The enemy would shoot an officer given the chance sooner than he would a regular soldier. It takes away their leadership, and you increase your goal. You create chaos in the ranks. However, it has been said that army sergeants are the backbone of any army. It takes an officer to say what needs to be done, but it takes a sergeant to see what needs done that it gets done. The difference is immense. Many a detail has been commanded by sergeants and a few men. Depending on the detail and the situation, a sergeant in charge is all that is needed.

Sergeant Dickerson, then reported, "There are ten to twenty Apache ahead of the detail, Lieutenant. They seem to know we're coming, but they're not in too big a hurry to attack, for some reason."

Lieutenant Lundstrom, then said, "How close would you say they are, Sergeant?"

Sergeant Dickerson replied, "Less than a mile, Sir. They just seem to be waiting for us."

The lieutenant then said, "Mister Grayson told me a Chiricahua sub-chief named, She'-te-quah, has 20 to 30 Apache behind us as well. So, then this, sub-chief, She'-te-quah, believes he has the detail in a trap?"

Sergeant Dickerson looked at Ned Grayson, causing Ned to answer, "It would seem so, Lieutenant. He does have us out numbered."

The lieutenant replied, "Yes, he does. We'll just outrun him then. If at all possible, we'll all come out of this alive." He rode to the wagon saying, "Lieutenant Murtaugh, hand each man a weapon, Sir. They may not be able to sit a horse, but they can fire a weapon."

2nd Lieutenant Murtaugh replied, "Yes, Sir."

Lieutenant Murtaugh turned, going back into the wagon. He took a crowbar and opened a crate of rifles.

He handed each man a brand new Henry repeating rifle, and a box of ammunition.

Each man took their rifle and marveled at the new weapon. Each man handled their new weapon with kid gloves, and admiring the look of it. Smiles all around.

In his distinct Scottish dialect, Jax MacDougall, then said, "Now, this is what we needed when we were attacked by those savages, Lieutenant. Ha, ha, ha, we would a showed 'em what for if we would a had these."

Then, Ernie Post said, "Agreed, Corporal Scotch…"

Jax butted in, "That's Scots, not Scotch. Scotch is a whisky. Are ye daft?"

Ernie replied, "Aw, Mac, you know what I meant."

Jax laughed, then said, "Now, we can give those savages what for, Lads."

Clint Fairfield replied, "This is just what the doctor ordered." Kissing the rifle on the fore stock, ending with a loud smack, he said, "Where have you been all my life?"

Lieutenant Lundstrom yelled out, "Whenever you're ready, Lieutenant Murtaugh. Let me know, and we'll move out slowly, then we'll give 'er hell, and run right through those Indians. We'll scare the 'B' Jesus out of 'em." He turned to Jamie asking, "Are you ready, Lieutenant?"

Jamie replied, "As I'll ever be, Lieutenant."

The 1st lieutenant, then said, "Mister Grayson, take the point."

Without a word, Ned Grayson, Army scout, reined his horse away from the 1st Lieutenant, and Sergeant Major, and took the point, out in front of the detail. Jax, Clint, and Ernie loaded their new Henry rifles, and had them at the ready. 16 rounds per rifle. One in the chamber, and 15 in the magazine. 30 to 40 rounds fired per minute can cut the size of the enemy down quite considerable if firing is precise and on target. But of course, we are talking about the Army, ain't we? (I'll just clear my throat and move on). Lieutenant Lundstrom pulled his service revolver from its holster, as did Jamie. 2nd Lieutenant, Adam Murtaugh regained his seat on the wagon box,

As he cradled a new loaded Henry rifle in the crook of his arm, he yelled out, "We're ready, Lieutenant, whenever you are!"

Lieutenant Lundstrom, then hollered, "All right, Lieutenant. Let's move out. Slow and easy as we go."

Private Spencer Ellsworth slapped the reins over the backs of the draft horses. The wagon lurched backwards, then gained a steady forward motion after rocking over uneven ground. Unbeknownst to 1st Lieutenant Miles Lundstrom, and the Whitesboro detail, they were about to run into something they had no idea would happen.

As the detail neared the mark that Sergeant Major Dickerson had said the Apache were waiting for the detail, Lieutenant Lundstrom yelled out, "Let's go!"

Private Spencer Ellsworth slapped the reins hurriedly over the horses' backs, yelling, "Yo, giddy-up there! He-yah! He-yah!"

The wagon picked up speed as the horses eventually reached full gallop while they pulled the wagon as it rushed along. The desert air rushed through the covered canvas of the wagon, which caused an air draft through the wagon causing various, assorted items to float in the air and, then fly out through the rear of the wagon to be lost on the wind.

Dust and dirt, and assorted sticks and small gravel flew up around the wheels as it hurried along on uneven ground, pitching one way, then another. Yet, the Apache had not attacked, which mystified Lieutenant Lundstrom, Sergeant Major Del Dickerson and Ned Grayson, scout. Neither man could explain it. What were the Apache waiting for? As Lieutenant Lundstrom slowed the detail, Ned turned on his saddle, looking down their back trail.

He, then said, "She'-te-quah is one shrewd customer, Lieutenant. This tactic is new, even for me."

Sergeant Major Dickerson, then said, "I don't get it either, Lieutenant. Where could they have gone, and what was their reason for goin'?"

Lieutenant Lundstrom replied, "I wouldn't know, Sergeant, but let's not dilly-dally, and look a gift horse in the mouth." Turning to Lieutenant Murtaugh, he hollered, "Let's go, Lieutenant! Move out!"

Again, the horses pulled against their harnesses and slowly reached full gallop. The wagon pitched one way, then the other. The troopers in the wagon were pitched one way, then the other.

Corporal Jax MacDougall yelled out over the noise of the wagon wheels, "With this pitching goin' on we'd lucky to hit the side of a barn."

Private Ernie Post, then said, "I keep reaching for my head, but I can't find it."

Then, came the usual sound of an Indian attack, the warbling sound of the war cry. The sound came from behind them on their rear trail. All four men turned their horses to face the rear as the wagon hurriedly rolled on ahead of them.

Lieutenant Lundstrom said, "We must a caught 'em asleep, but here they come."

All four men reined their horses to catch the wagon. Lieutenant Lundstrom caught up to the driver side of the wagon.

The lieutenant hollered up at Private Spencer Ellsworth, "Let's get this rig movin', Private! We'll do our best at a skirmish line and afford you some cover fire."

The fear on 2nd Lieutenant Adam Murtaugh's face was plain enough. All he could do was stare wide-eyed out into space. He seemed to be froze in one place. Lieutenant Lundstrom pulled on his horses' reins to fall back behind the wagon. He shouted orders for a skirmish line. The four men reined in at close quarters to one another facing their rear, and the oncoming Indian war party.

Lieutenant Lundstrom, the hollered, "On my command!"

Sergeant Major Dickerson then hollered, "They're not in range, Lieutenant!"

"Then, this will give them something to look forward to"

As the Apache war party came closer, Lieutenant Lundstrom hollered, "Ready! Aim! Fire!"

The roar of gunfire was chaotic noise. And, again, the Lieutenant gave the command.

"Ready! Aim! Fire!"

And, again, the roar of gunfire was chaotic noise. Then, all four men reined their horses in an effort to catch the wagon. Then, out of nowhere, there came the sound of a bugle. Fain't, but definitely heard over the roar of the wagon wheels. 2nd Lieutenant Murtaugh turned his head to the sound of the bugle.

Lieutenant Murtaugh, then said, "You hear that, Private? That's a bugle. It's sounding the charge!"

Private Ellsworth hollered back, "Yes, Sir. I hear it!"

Then, Lieutenant Murtaugh began to laugh a maniacal laugh of lunacy. Private Ellsworth looked at Lieutenant Murtaugh in a serious look of surprise, mixed with astonishment.

Chapter Seven

Different

The two squads of troopers came charging from the right side of the detail.

Lieutenant Lundstrom then ordered that Ned Grayson and Sergeant Major Dickerson stay with the wagon, while he and Jamie join the troopers to afford a defense of this Indian attack. The officer in charge of the two squads was a man that Lieutenant Lundstrom knew all too well. It was 1st Lieutenant, Micah Chapman from the Comanche patrol. Meaning the rest of the troop under command of Captain Gary Locke was close by. 1st Lieutenant Lundstrom had gladly surrendered his command to 1st Lieutenant Micah Chapman. They shortly exclaimed their cordial pleasantries, then they got to the business at hand. An attacking Apache war party.

1st Lieutenant Chapman ordered a staggard skirmish line. The troopers were equipped with the newest Henry repeating rifle. There were two rows of troopers. The back row was staggard from the front row as to not shoot the man in front of them. As the Apache war party came screaming closer to the re-enforced Whitesboro detail, the troopers held their fire for them to come a little closer. When the Apache war party got about a hundred yards from the re-enforced detail, 1st Lieutenant Micah Chapman gave the command.

"Ready! Aim! Fire!"

The impact from the first volley of rifle fire was very effective.

A lot of Indian ponies balked squealing, pitching their wounded, or dead riders into the dirt to lay still.

Micah, then commanded the second row of troopers, "Ready! Aim! Fire!"

Again, the same effect. Wounded, or dead Apache were strewn across a wide area.

Miles shouted, "That took the fight out of 'em! Look at 'em run!"

As they watched the Apache break and run from the field of battle, there came a cheer of victory from the troopers.

Jamie said, "That's the best thing I've seen all year, Lieutenant."

Lieutenant Lundstrom replied, "You'll get no argument from me, Lieutenant."

Micah, then said, "No need to chase them. There isn't enough of them left to worry 'bout. At least for now there isn't."

Jamie, then said, "From what I've learned while bein' out here is this, even one Apache is too many. They know how to kill you 50 ways from sundown."

Micah replied, "You're quite right, Lieutenant. The only Indian tribe to put the Apache on the run has been the Comanche. But when it comes to an Apache himself, I found there's none meaner than the Tonto Apache. He's meaner than a coiled rattlesnake."

Miles said, "Man am I glad to see you, Micah. Where did you come from? My God," He laughed joyfully. "I thought we were goin' to die."

"It's good to see you alive, Miles. Glad we could be of help. We've had our run ins with Indians ourselves ever since we left the Lake Texoma area where the Comanche massacre took place. We were attacked by the Kiowa. We came away with the bodies of Captain Philo Dobbs, 1st Lieutenant, Jeffery Welch, also 2nd Lieutenant, Andrew Dumbrowski, and 1st Sergeant, Gene Ralston. There are many more on the five wagons, but then, there were so many we couldn't identify, so we buried them where they laid. Horrible duty, Miles. Just plain Horrible."

Miles replied, "Now, I feel plum horrible, Micah. From what you just told me, I've had the easy duty. Bring those men who survived that Comanche massacre back to Ringgold Barracks."

Micah, then said, "A detail worth doing, Miles. They deserve recognition for their bravery in escaping a Comanche massacre, and live to tell about their harrowing experience."

Miles replied, "I don't quite see it the way you do, I guess. All those men did was survive a massacre, and that's all they did."

Micah, then asked, "Well, don't you think that deserves recognition"

"Recognition, yes, but displayed as heroes, and most likely getting medals for it, no, I don't. They were just lucky is all, and that's all there is to it. Pure dumb luck."

Micah said, "That's your duty to perform, Miles, and who said anything about heroes?"
Miles replied, "My duty, yes. Doesn't mean I have to like it."

Lieutenant Chapman turned from Lieutenant Lundstrom shaking his head with a brand new understanding of who 1st Lieutenant Miles Lundstrom is. A no nonsense kind of man with a high and mighty attitude of himself with no compassion, or empathy for his fellow man, especially those of a lower rank than himself.

Then, Captain Locke and the rest of the troop, and the five wagons came onto the scene. Captain Locke was joined by Lieutenant Chapman, Lieutenant Lundstrom, and Jamie.

Captain Locke looked at Jamie saying, "I take it you are 2nd Lieutenant Carlson?"

"Yes, Sir. From Ringgold Barracks, Captain."

Captain Locke, then said, "I'm sorry you had to go through that, Lieutenant. It must've been such a misery for you. But I am impressed with your tenacity to continue, and command your detail to cover open ground to Whitesboro, and gain medical aid for your men."

Jamie replied, "Thank you, Sir. It was either that, or die from starvation, and thirst."

Captain Locke smiled, then asked, "Am I to understand that that is the wagon carrying the rest of your detail, Lieutenant?"

"Yes, Sir."

Captain Locke asked, "Who are the three riding horses?"

Jamie answered, "That would be Sergeant Major Del Dickerson, and Army scout, Ned Grayson, Captain, and of course, Sergeant Everett Sutrell, Sir."

Lieutenant Lundstrom, then said, "There is 2nd Lieutenant Adam Murtaugh, who is a physician's assistant on the wagon, Sir, along with Private, Spencer Ellsworth at the reins, and Corporal Frank Sande, plus myself, Captain. 1st Lieutenant Miles Lundstrom, Sir."

Captain Locke, then said, "Well, Lieutenant Lundstrom, you've done a fine job. You demand a well-deserved recognition as well as those men. I hope that recognition comes in the form of a citation of a job well done, Sir. You may not know it, Lieutenant, but you have done a great service to the Army of the United States by bringing those men back to their command."

Lieutenant Lundstrom replied, "You, yourself, Captain, have done no small feat, Sir."

Captain Locke said, "It was my duty, Sir. A duty that was unmistakably a humbling, and reverent duty. Recovery of bodies of the men you served with, and honored to walk beside."

Lieutenant Lundstrom replied, "But Captain, it was your duty, Sir."

"Yes, Lieutenant, my duty. I agree it was no small feat, but that duty needed done. I played the hand that was dealt me. I hated it. Even now, I hate it."

Lieutenant Lundstrom, then said, "I'm sorry you feel that way, Sir."

Captain Locke looked at Lieutenant Lundstrom with surprise.

Captain Locke asked, "Just how should I feel 'bout that duty, Lieutenant?"

"I don't know, Captain. No disrespect meant, but I know how I'd feel."

"I'm sure what we feel differently, Lieutenant, is just that. Different."

Flynn, Seamus, and Clancy mounted their horses and reined them away from Deeb's Livery, and nosed them out of town towards the pecan orchard where Timothy McFadden, and Kevin Taylor are waiting with the wagon of weapons. Unbeknownst to those three men, one of Brass Tacks men had just left the Etsy barn checking wagons and their loads when he saw them ride down main street. The man quickly mounted his horse, and hurriedly went to the Dancing Bear saloon to let Brass Tacks know what he had seen. When the man entered the Dancing Bear saloon, he found Lane with Lilah Silko sitting on his lap, giggling, and carrying on like school children.

It took a few seconds for the man to say anything, but he knew he had to.

The man, then said, "Lane, I saw 'em. I saw 'em, Lane. They was ridin' down main street."

Lane casually asked, "You saw who, Rex?"

Rex Tibbs replied, "Them Irishmen you're after. Ridin' plain as day down main street."

Lane hurried to his feet, dumping Lilah as he did to the floor to land on her butt. She shrieked when her butt hit the floor, then she gave Lane a look of contempt.

Ignoring Lilah, Lane asked, "How long ago."

Rex answered, "No more 'n two minutes ago. I got here as soon as I could."

Lane questioned, "Which way they headed?"

Rex replied, "You know them pecan trees we passed coming into town?"

Lane replied, "Yeah. So?"

 Rex, then said, "They went that way."

Lane scoffed, then said, "Still don't know your east from west, eh, Rex?"

"Maybe I don't, Lane, but I know which way they was goin'."

As Lilah got to her feet, Lane hollered, "Get to your horses!"

As Lane and his men ran from the saloon, Lilah stomped her feet as she yelled out, "Lane!?"

Mateo looked on in surprise at the goings on, saying, "Ay, caramba!"

Herschel came in from another room as Lilah screamed after Lane.

Herschel turned to Mateo asking, "What did you say to them, Mateo?"

Mateo replied, "Who? Me? I said nothing, Senior." He done the sign of the cross saying, "I swear I said nothing, I think."

Herschel asked Lilah, "What happened?"

Still a little miffed, she answered, "I don't know. Something 'bout some Irishmen, and off they went for whatever reason."